THE BLAKE BROTHERS

Kathey Gray

The Blake Brothers : a novel / by: Kathey Gray

This book is dedicated to my parents, who always encouraged me to chase my dreams. My husband, who always supports me in all my colors. My kids, who put up with my obsession with fantastical characters. And lastly, my brothers.

"There is a charm about the forbidden that makes it unspeakably desirable." - Mark Twain

CHAPTER ONE

Portland

I still remember the moment I knew my life was going to change immensely. I had just got off the bus from school. It was early April, not that you could tell. Springtime in Minnesota wasn't exactly bees buzzing and flowers in full bloom. Barging through the front door, I took off my jacket and hung it up on the coat rack. I slid the beanie off of my blonde hair and tossed it on the kitchen table. I cupped my hands together and tried to warm them by breathing into them. I went to raid the fridge, my usual after school routine. Since there wasn't much to chose from in there, I checked the freezer. I found a box of pepperoni hot pockets. My stomach growled angrily at the site of them. The box was opened, so I took one out unwrapped it, slipped on its sleeve and set in on the paper plate. I popped it in the microwave and went to grab a Coke out of the fridge while I waited for my food. When the microwave beeped, I took my food out and sat down to eat, trying not to burn my tongue. *That was the moment.* I heard my parents talking in the living room in hushed voices.

Something about the way they were speaking, caused me to pause and listen closer.

"We need to tell her soon...*today.*" I heard my dad say, he sounded stoic.

"I know," I heard my mom sigh. "How do think she'll *take* it?" She sounded concerned.

"Doesn't matter. We have no choice," he said, gruffly.

I had a strange feeling twisting in my stomach. That night my parents sat me down and told me we were moving. My dad had lost his job and had been offered a job by my uncle John, in Portland. We were moving this summer, as soon as I finished the ninth grade. I was excited and scared. Pemberton was where I was born and raised. I'd miss my friends, but I'd always wanted to see more of the world.

* * *

The next month flew by fast and before I knew it, it was time to pack up the U-haul and say our goodbyes. Luckily, we didn't actually have many things, we never had. We were okay with that, we didn't need the finer things to be happy. I said goodbye to my best friend since Kindergarten, Riley. She hugged me tightly and almost choked me.

"Promise you'll text and Face-Time me as much as you can?" She pleaded with me.

"I promise," I smiled.

She seemed satisfied with my answer because she let go of my neck and held me at arms length. She smiled at me wistfully, then punched me on the arm. "You *better*."

I laughed. "Riley, I will *literally* know *no one* there. *Trust me*, I'll be blowing up your phone. You're going to get sick of me." We laughed together with tears in our eyes.

We embraced one last time and I hopped into the truck with my parents. I waved goodbye to Riley and looked toward the road, toward my future.

We left in the evening and drove straight through, only stopping for gas and food. It was a long drive, but I couldn't complain too much, it was quite scenic.

The next evening, as the sun was setting, we finally turned onto our new street. I was immediately astonished at how beautiful the trees were. The houses on our street were sort of shabby looking, but their nostalgic appearance gave them charm. When we pulled into our driveway, I noticed that our new house could definitely use some work, also. It only looked slightly abandoned, but I knew my mom could clean it up nice.

My mom stepped out of the truck first, inhaling dramatically. "*Wow!* Can you *smell* that fresh air?" She turned and grinned widely at me and my dad.

I hid my smirk, knowing that she was just trying to stay positive, even though our new house looks like a dump. My dad got out next, smiling too. I watched as my mom ran up and unlocked the front door with our new key, yelling at us to come see. But my dad is all business, he opens the back of the U-haul and begins unloading boxes. Scout, my Golden Retriever, hops out after me. Suddenly, I heard loud rock music playing. I turned to see a black SUV pull into the drive next to us.

My dad glances over his shoulder and shakes his head, grumbling. "Our new *neighbors*, I presume."

I watched four guys get out of the SUV and I note that they're all teenagers, brothers perhaps. They seem to be ranging in all ages and don't look exactly alike. The biggest and eldest no doubt, looked sort of scary with his tattooed arms and shaved-bald head. I continued to study them one by one. The two behind the scary drew my attention next. One of them was skinny and the other of medium build. They both had stark black hair. I watched them curiously. They didn't even seem to *notice* me, as they carried on joking and laughing with each other. The last one stepped out, he caught my attention the most. His hair is dirty blonde and his build is lean and muscular. He looks about my age and very handsome, incidentally. His demeanor seems different than the others, he seems quiet. For some reason, he *does* notice me. He pauses and looks over at me, his eyebrows furrowing. Our eyes meet, mine hazel and his light blue. Scout starts growling at my side. I turn my attention to her momentarily, reaching down to pet her head to calm her, but when I look back up, he's gone. They all retreated into their house.

"C'mon Scout," I encourage her and head inside to see my new home.

Inside, the house resembles that of one in a horror movie. The old wooden floors are scratched up and a few windows are broken in the living room and kitchen. Tattered curtains sway in the evening breeze. There's a few pieces of outdated furniture; a couch and a table and chairs. The house smells ancient and everything is covered in a thick layer of dust. Scout sneezes next to me. My mom has already set to work sweeping the floors. My dad moves in and out of the house, unloading boxes.

My mom looks up at me. "Why don't you go check out your room, hun? It's down the hall at the end."

I nod and do as she says. The door opens with a long creak. My room isn't the biggest but it has a connected bathroom. It doesn't have a shower, but it does have a large, old-fashioned bath tub. It has an old, twin-sized bed with a brass-colored bed frame. The sheets are outdated and smell like dust. I pull my tattered curtain aside, and am happy to see that at least *my* window isn't broken. I gasp when I find myself staring straight at the handsome boy who was outside earlier. My room is a direct view of his. His back is turned to me, thankfully, so he doesn't know that I'm watching him. Suddenly, he lifts the hem of his shirt and pulls it over his head. Now I *know* I'm snooping, but I can't look away. I'm shocked when I spot a huge tattoo in the middle of his back. It looks like some sort of a weird symbol that I can't decipher. He bends down to grab something in front of him.

Weights?

He starts to lift them and I can see every muscle in his back flex, some that I didn't even know *existed*. I close the curtain, too shame-faced to keep looking.

Maybe he isn't as innocent as he looks?

He looks *way* too young to have a tattoo, especially of that *size?* My parents would *kill* me. I head back into the living room to see what my parents are doing, and to try to distract myself from what I just saw. I find my mom dusting, my dad is already passed out on the couch.

My mom looks up at me when I enter the room. Her short blonde hair is pulled back into a ponytail. A few stray pieces fall into her face. She brushes them away. "So, what do you think. Livable?" she asks, her brown eyes wide.

I look up, trying to fight the smile off of my face. "*Totally livable.*"

That summer went by quickly. Weeks are spent fixing up our house. Painting, replacing floorboards and broken windows. Also, a *lot* of cleaning. My parents work and I stay home with Scout. We spend the weekends discovering the city. I admire the boy from next door from afar, wondering if he'll go to my school. Before I know it, it's August, time to start at my new school.

CHAPTER TWO

First Impressions

When I wake for my first day of school, both of my parents had already left for work. My dad, to a factory in town with my uncle; my mom, waitressing at a local diner. Unfortunately for me, that would mean I'd either have to *walk* or ride my bike to school. We only have one vehicle to share, and it was currently with my mom. My parents worked it out though, they made sure to pick a house close to a high school. It was only one block away, but nonetheless humiliating for me.

I decided to go for the bike, since I was running late to school, on my *first* day. I was about to round the corner to the front of the school, when I spotted the big SUV whip around into the parking lot. I stopped short, waiting to watch the group of burly boys exit the vehicle. I didn't want *him* to see me. They all get out and I spy him. His hair is slicked back and he's wearing a brown jacket, rugged jeans and brown boots. I watched as they all entered the front of the school. Then I rushed over, chaining my bike to the rack, and half run inside. Portland High is huge and I blend in easily. No one seems to notice me or know that I'm new. I go into the front office to retrieve my schedule. I look over it quickly and feel the panic rising in my chest.

Oh no, why am I in Algebra II? I'm *terrible* at Math!

To make matters worse, it's *first* period. I realize I don't have time to settle this matter today without being late, so I read the room number and make my way there. My stomach is in knots as I take a seat right before the first bell rings. The teacher begins writing on the blackboard. I take out my spiral and begin taking notes that I will most definitely be needing. The door opens abruptly.

Of all people, I think. It's *him* again, my attractive neighbor.

The teacher, a man of slight build that looks like he's barely in his twenties, turns slightly and calls over his shoulder. "Late again, Mr. Blake?"

He says nothing, just smirks and walks past the teacher's desk. The girls seem to sit straighter in their seats at the sight of him. I'm glad I'm not the *only* one who seems to fancy him. He walks down the row of seats and stops in front of, *me?* He stands above me, staring. My heart is pounding in my chest. My cheeks are growing red.

What the hell is he doing?

I look up reluctantly, to meet his unavoidable gaze. *"Yes?"* I mutter, awkwardly.

"You're in my seat," he smirks, amused, his clear, blue eyes assessing me.

He's even *more* handsome up close. His skin is clear, he has straight, white, perfect teeth, long curly eyelashes and dimples. I'm pleasantly surprised when I detect an Irish lilt to his voice.

I wonder if he's an exchange student?

"Oh...*sorry.*" My face flames. I begin to gather my things, hurriedly, when the teacher's voice stops me.

"Oh, of course! How could I *forget?* We have a new student! Class, this is Abigail Brooks, I want you all to be *very* welcoming to her."

My face turns beet red as all eyes turn towards me. I half-wave, awkwardly.

"I'm Mr. Tyler and we *do* have assigned seats, but you can sit there today, because Benjamin here, was just headed to the principal's office for being tardy *again,*" he informs me.

The girls in the class smile and giggle. The guys snicker, too. Benjamin rolls his eyes and heads back to the door, pushing it open a little too roughly.

The rest of my classes are uneventful. I repeat the same uncomfortable routine of being introduced as the new girl. I make friends with a girl named Meghan, a pale, red-headed girl in my English class, who helps me find my way around for the remainder of the day. I don't see Benjamin again though, which I'm way too disappointed about. That bothers me.

After school, I walk out the front doors and am horrified to see that it's raining. Not just a sprinkle, it's *pouring*. I pull up my hoodie and make a mad dash across the yard. By the time I get to my bike, I'm already soaked. My hands slip as I fumble with my bike lock. I curse to myself until I get it unlocked. I hop onto the soaking wet seat and ride my way through the rain. I spot the SUV again and decide to take an alley, in hopes that I won't get recognized. The rain is merciless though and I can barely see through my blurry eyes. I slosh through the puddles in record speed, trying to beat the SUV. I'm almost home when my front tire hits something. A large rock, causes my bike to swerve. I get flung off my bike in one swift motion and my bike lands on top of me. I'm too hurt to cuss this time. Rain is hitting my face hard, like pellets. My limbs feel so cold, like I have no blood running through them. I untangle my legs from my bike. I notice my jeans are ripped on the knee and I check to see if I'm bleeding. I have a small cut. I assess the rest of my injuries, but they're just bruises. I pick up my bike, no longer in a hurry. I note that the tire is deflated.

Stupid rock. *Great*. Now I'll have to walk the rest of the way home.

"Need some help with that?" I hear a familiar voice say.

I don't even have to look up to know who it is, but I do anyway. Benjamin is standing proudly, shoulders tall, with his hands in his pockets, looking ever the superhero. He's smiling an adorable smile and his eyes are twinkling with amusement.

"*How?* How did you know I was *here*, Benjamin?" I stammer, stupidly, feeling a thrill run through my body at the sound of his name out of my own lips for the first time.

"I *saw* you...you looked like you were having a hard time," he tries to fight a smile.

I'm dying of embarrassment and I don't look too hot at the moment, either. Plus it's the *second* time I've felt like an idiot in front of him. But who's keeping score?

"Well, you came a little too late, I'm almost home." I walk past him, stubbornly pushing my bike.

He jogs up next to me. "At least let me help you with your bike," he offers gently.

It surprises me, and for some reason I let him take it from my hands. His fingers brush against mine. Mine are like ice and his are warm.

"Are you hurt?" he asks, concern in his voice. Shock runs through me at the gentleness in his tone.

"No, I'm fine," I grimace, too humiliated to admit that I am.

He eyes my knee skeptically, but doesn't say anything. We walk in silence in the rain until we get to my front porch. He leans the bike against the brick wall.

"Thanks, Benjamin," I say, sincerely.

He even looks good bathed in the ugly fluorescent lighting on my front porch.

"No problem...see you at school," he says, suddenly serious.

"Okay," I reply, weakly.

He half turns, but then faces me again. "Oh, and it's *Ben*. No one calls me by my full name," he smirks.

"Okay, Ben. I go by Abby, nice to meet you," I say, extending my hand for him to shake.

He looks at it, bemused, but shakes it anyway. "You too," he smirks.

For some reason, we hold hands for too long. I hear someone call him and he lets go of my hand, abruptly.

"Bye, Ben."

"Bye," he says shortly, before hurrying off.

I watch him as he crosses the yard and disappears from my sight.

* * *

My parents aren't home from work yet, so the house is dark and creepy. I flick on the lights on my way to my room. I head straight to the bathroom, shivering convulsively. I turn on the faucet in the bath tub, and it stutters and groans. I realize that it probably hasn't been turned on in a while, I've been using my parent's shower all summer. The faucet spews out black water, which startles me.

"*Ew!*" I say to myself, horrified.

But after the water runs for a minute, it clears and I'm relieved. I put the stopper in and fill the tub with steaming water. I peel off my soaked clothes and ease into the tub. After I'm clean and the heat has been sufficiently restored to my body, I get out and wrap myself in a towel. I change into my PJ's and sit down on my bed. I notice the sheets have been changed, my mom must've done that sometime. Maybe she came home on her lunch break? I grab the book I was reading last and resume reading. Suddenly, I hear loud voices yelling. I lean forward, trying to find out where it's coming from. Then I realize it's coming from Benjamin's house. I peek through the curtain to see if I can see anything, but they must be in another room.

"What did I tell you?" A booming voice scolds.

I hear a voice that sounds like Ben's, respond quietly, but I can't make out his response.

"Leave things alone. Leave her alone. You know the rules. I'm serious." The voice says.

I realize that it must be Ben's brother's voice that I hear, because he has the same Irish accent, only thicker. Ben says something again, but it's unintelligible. Then everything gets quiet, I assume that the argument is over.

That was strange, I think to myself.

I'm sure that couldn't have had anything to do *me*, right? That'd be *crazy*. All he did was help me. Was he some sort of strange religion that didn't allow interaction with girls? Surely not. Before I can analyze the situation more, I hear the front door open. My parents are home.

"Abby, I brought home burgers from the diner!" My mom calls.

My stomach growls. "*Coming, mom*," I call back.

CHAPTER THREE
Walls

I had to walk to school the next morning because of my popped bike tire. I didn't really mind too much, and thank goodness it wasn't raining yet. Although, the clouds appeared dark and heavy with rain, so I knew it would only a matter of time until it did. I came prepared though, I wore my gray rain jacket and tall, brown boots. I wasn't sure if I'd see Ben today, since I hadn't been to all of my classes yet. I got to school early somehow and had time to arrange my things in my locker. I saw Ben and his brothers emerge from the end of the hallway. They all walked together, like some sort of bad boy, Irish gang. If I was being honest, they *did* look intimidating.

Meghan skipped up next to me all of a sudden. "What'cha looking at, newbie?"

Caught staring, I turned quickly and pretended to be getting a book. "*Nothing*," I replied.

"That didn't *look* like *nothing*," she pried, her lips quirking up in a smile. "In *fact*," she continued, "that looked a lot like you were looking at the Blake brothers." She waggled her brows at me.

I scoffed. *"The Blake brothers?* Why do you say it like they're some sort of *gang?*"

She snickers next to me. "You could say that."

I raise my eyebrows at her.

There is something strange about them...

"The oldest one, Max, is like their 'leader'. He's already been to jail a few times and he's covered in tattoos, even though he's barely a senior."

I feel my eyebrows creep even higher on my face.

Meghan continues, "I saw him beat the crap out of some guy one time at a party, it was *scary*. He beat that dude to a bloody pulp. No one messes with him, they call him 'Max, bloody-fists, Blake'."

My eyes are popping out of my head now. "And the others?" I inquire, dying of curiosity.

She smirks, pleased with herself. "The second eldest, Joseph, is not to be underestimated either, he just has less of a temper. Quinn is more of a thief, but I heard he's got a crazy streak." I listen on, captivated, watching the brothers walk down the hall.

"And the youngest?" I feel myself holding my breath.

"Oh," she breathes, "pretty-boy Benjamin? He's no angel either. Playboy, con-artist...he'll steal your heart and your parents' bank account before you even know what hit you."

I gape.

She pauses and touches her pointer finger to her lips, pondering. "You know...that might make him the *most* dangerous of them all."

"*Dangerous?*" I breathe, astonished.

"We'd better get to class," she informs me.

I grab my things and shut my locker, stalking after her. "How...*dangerous*...are they?"

She raises her eyebrows at me. "Everyone who has half a brain keeps their distance from the Blake brothers...except for, you know, *groupies.*"

"*Oh,*" I breathe.

"Yeah. Trouble seems to sort of, *follow them.*"

I'm lost in my own thoughts.

Meghan nudges me. "Hey, see you at lunch, okay?"

"Okay," I mutter and walk to class.

Of course he's trouble, I think to myself.

But he was so sweet to me the other day...he can't be all bad, right? The word "*playboy*" runs through my head.

Well, he isn't going to be playing me, I think.

I don't see Ben in my Spanish or Chemistry classes. At lunch, I head to the table where Meghan sits. I test my food, experimentally. I'm surprised how good the cafeteria food is here. I'm introduced to more people, and they all seem nice. I look up and see Ben walk to a table and sit by himself. Some part of me feels sorry for him, sitting alone. I have the urge to go keep him company. I get up in the middle of a conversation about people who are Instagram famous. Meghan glances over at me for a moment, but must assume I'm done eating. I walk over to Ben's table and sit down. He looks shocked initially, but recovers quickly.

"Hi," I say and go about eating like nothing's wrong.

"...*Hi*," he mutters and looks around him.

We eat in silence for a moment.

"What's wrong, new friends boring you?" he smirks.

I shake my head. "Just thought you could use some company."

"I *bet* you did," he smirks, but his eyes are guarded.

I furrow my brows trying to figure him out. He's acting different than yesterday. Although, unfortunately, just as handsome. He's wearing a fitted, black t-shirt that shows off his muscles and his usually tame hair is wilder today, almost spiky. He's wearing a thin, silver chain around his neck. His blue eyes slice through me and make me wish I hadn't come. Suddenly, a girl with bleach blonde hair comes and sits in his lap and giggles. Behind her, comes a raven-haired girl, who sits beside him. She whispers something into his ear. They both ignore me, as if I'm not sitting right there. I'd be jealous if the girls didn't look so trashy.

He keeps his eyes on me and smiles broadly. "See, I have *plenty* of company."

I glare at him, disgusted, then shake my head. "Whatever," I say, getting up with my tray. I turn and walk to the dumpster, dumping my food inside.

I've *completely* lost my appetite. I guess I know what Meghan meant now about his "groupies". Maybe I *do* need to stay away from him and his brothers. Maybe the glimpse of goodness I thought I saw in him was just an act he uses on girls.

The next two classes are miserable. I don't know why I'm so disappointed, Benjamin Blake didn't owe me anything. After school, I start walking home.

"*Hey, Abby!*" I hear my name being called. I turn to see Meghan hanging her head out of her boyfriend's truck.

"Hey, Meg!" I smile and wave.

"You want a ride home?" She offers.

"Sure!" I say.

Suddenly, I feel myself being lifted off of my feet. My heart feels like it falls into my stomach.

"I got her," says a warm voice behind me. I turn to look at the person carrying me and am stunned to see that he's gorgeous. He's tall and has brown, curly hair and green eyes.

"Jamie! Oh my gosh! Put her *down!*" Meghan chokes out, laughing hysterically.

I notice we're causing a scene, everyone is looking our way, staring, including Ben. But 'Jamie' loads me into the truck as if I weigh nothing, then climbs in next to me.

"Hi, I'm Jamie" He extends his hand to me.

I take it, awkwardly. "I heard," I smile.

"Jamie, you goofball," Meghan laughs.

"I'm Abby, but you already know that too." I pull my hand from his.

"I know, I've heard all about you," he beams.

What has he heard?

His happiness is contagious though, I find myself in a better mood already.

"So kids," he says conspiratorially. "What sort of trouble do you want to get into tonight?"

"I thought we were going home?" I ask Meghan.

She smiles a sneaky smile. "Only if you *want* to?"

I think about what happened today with Ben. "No, I don't," I decide.

"Okay," says Aiden, Meghan's boyfriend. "The cabin it is."

Kathey Gray

CHAPTER FOUR

The Cabin

Aiden likes rap a lot. Jay Z, in particular. It bumps through the radio speakers as we head up a winding road, into the forest. There are so many trees, I almost get dizzy, watching them blur past. We approach a small cabin, where it looks like the party's already started. I see a bunch of kids from my school there already. I peek my head up to see if Ben's here. Not that I should *want* him to be there...

"Looking for someone?" Jamie inquires.

"Oh...no. I've never been here before, it looks...*fun*," I say, not sounding the least bit excited.

Aiden parks the truck.

"Well *c'mon* then!" Jamie grabs my hand, pulling me out of the truck.

"Jamie, if you keep *bothering* the girl, you're going to scare her away," Aiden teases.

I flush, looking down.

I can't help but notice the similarities between Jamie and Aiden. They both are tall and have a curly, mop of hair. Only Jamie's hair is dark brown, not blonde, and Aiden's eyes are blue, not green.

Jamie laughs. "I'm not scaring you, *am I?*" he jokes.

"*No*," I laugh, feeling awkward.

We walk up to the crowd and Meghan introduces me to more of her friends. I notice there is a keg and a lot of red cups being passed around. Every time one gets passed to me, I wait until no one's looking and spill it out. I'm glad to see that Aiden is responsible and is the designated driver for the night. I wish I could say the same for Meg. My supposed new best friend is quite the lush, downing cup after cup. When it gets dark, they spark up a bonfire and start roasting marshmallows. It smells amazing and the cool air is crisp. I sit on a log and stare at the fire. My thoughts wander to Benjamin. He's so confusing, sweet one moment, and cold the next. I wish I could figure him out. I text my mom and let her know that I'm alright and that I'm with Meg. Jamie comes to sit next to me.

"So how do you like Portland?"

"It's beautiful here," I sigh.

"But?"

"But *nothing.*" I shrink away from him.

"Oh, I get it, you're *shy*," he smiles.

I shrug. "I guess." *More like guarded, from overly-friendly, attractive strangers.*

He laughs, and it's a warm, comforting sound. He takes a pen out of his pocket and takes my hand, writing something in my palm. "Look, if you ever want to talk or hang out, that's my number," he smirks. I stare at my hand, not knowing what to say.

That was unexpected.

"*Time to go!*" Aiden yells. "*Meg's sick.*"

We both get up and get into the truck. On the way home, Meg rests her head on Aiden, sick as a dog. I wonder how she's going to be at school tomorrow, if she even *goes*.

We get to my house finally and Meg is passed out. I wave to Aiden and Jamie. I walk up to the front porch and see that my bike is still there, but something is *different*. I look closer and see that the tire's been fixed and is no longer flat. I reach down and squeeze it in awe. I smile and walk inside. I find that my parents are waiting up on me.

My mom is standing in the kitchen. "Hey hun," she says. "I made chicken pot pies, there's one for you in the oven."

"Thanks, mom."

"Did you have fun with Meghan?" she asks.

"Yeah," I respond shortly, not wanting to elaborate on the details.

"Hey, dad," I call to my dad, who's sitting in the living room watching TV.

"What's up, baby girl?" he asks, his dark green eyes glued to the game on the TV.

"Thanks for fixing my bike tire," I call, grabbing my chicken pot pie out of the oven.

"Hun, as much as I'd like to take credit for whatever you're talking about...that wasn't me," he answers, still distracted by the game.

I freeze. If my *dad* didn't fix it, then *who* did? I feel like I need to double check. I put down my food and walk into the living room.

"You didn't fix my bike tire?" I furrow my brows in confusion.

He looks up at me, furrowing his own dark brows back at me, mirroring the action. His brown hair is messy, he looks like he just woke up.

"No, you never told me anything was wrong with it. I can fix it tomorrow after work?" he suggests.

I pause, perplexed. "No...that's okay. It doesn't need to be fixed anymore."

My dad looks up at me, puzzled.

I heat up my chicken pot pie and take it to my room to eat it, without from my parents' curious eyes on me. I can't help but think, for some reason, that makes no sense at all...it was *Ben*.

CHAPTER FIVE

Red Flags

I ride my bike to school with butterflies in my stomach, I have no idea what to expect when I see Ben today in Algebra. Knowing the sweet gesture he did for me, but also learning some unfavorable things about him. I get to school, chain my bike up and head to my locker. While I'm there, I see Meg. She looks like she's seen better days. I wave to her and she waves back, looking chagrined. Not her usual chatty self today, I see. I walk to class alone.

"You're over here, Ms. Brooks," Mr. Tyler points at the seat beside Ben.

Ben looks up at me, meeting my eyes, then he looks back down again. I go take my seat. Mr. Tyler begins the lesson. I steal a few glances at Ben, but he keeps his head turned and his eyes trained forward.

So this is how he was going to play it?

I take a lot of notes and pay strict attention to keep my mind off of him. When the bell rings and we all shuffle out, I catch up to Ben.

"Thanks for fixing my bike tire," I huff.

He keeps walking fast. "I don't know what you're talking about," he mutters, smirking.

"*Really?*" I laugh, in disbelief.

He turns to me, and his eyes briefly flash with anger. "That's what I *said*, *isn't it?*" he snaps.

I feel like I've been punched in the stomach.

"Yeah...*right*," I fume. I turn and start walking in the opposite direction.

Ben catches my wrist and turns me back around. "I'm *sorry*, Abby," he pleads, his voice soft and his eyes devastatingly innocent.

Perplexed, I look down at my wrist. He realizes he's still holding onto it and drops it. "It's okay...Ben," I breathe.

"Maybe..." he starts. I wait. "Maybe we can eat lunch together today," he says, his face grave.

"Um...okay. Just *us?*" I ask, wondering what this all means. I'd rather eat lunch in the bathroom, than with his little, girl fan club around again.

"Yeah," he smirks, "*just us.*"

I can barely concentrate in my next classes, knowing that I'm going to be having lunch with Ben today....just us. I feel like something pivotal is going to happen, but only *he* understands what that is.

When I get to the cafeteria, my eyes scan the room, looking for him. I can't find him and I start to feel worried, when a disturbing thought crosses my mind.

What if he was just messing with me? What if he's doing this as a prank? Would he do that?

Just when I'm about to head to Meg's table to hang my head, I see him. He emerges from the lunch line with his tray and gestures me to sit at the table he usually sits at. He smiles mischievously at me, and I smile nervously back. Remembering my friend's words of warning, I take the seat opposite of him.

"You showed," he smiles.

"Yeah," I mutter.

Was he worried that I wouldn't?

We start eating in awkward silence.

"So why did you ask me to? Are your girlfriends sick today?" I blurt out, bravely.

He laughs quietly. "They're not my girlfriends."

I feel a tiny hope building inside of me, I know better but I can't help it.

"I'm as free as a bird," he leans back, putting his hands behind his head.

While I'm looking at him, I spot Jamie walking by, through the glass cafeteria windows, he sees me and waves frantically. I laugh and wave back. Ben looks behind him, something flashes in his eyes, *jealousy?*

"Friend of yours?" he asks, in a mock bored tone.

"Yeah," I smirk.

"*Actually*, I asked you to eat with me because, I thought, maybe, we could be friends...secretly." His eyebrows pulled together.

"What do you mean *secretly?* We're in public right now," I ask, confounded.

"With a few exceptions," he allowed.

"*Lunch* being an exception?" I raise a brow. I wonder to myself if that's because none of his brothers have lunch with him.

He doesn't want them to know? I guessed to myself.

I didn't see any of them around. They must all be in a grade above him.

"Yes," he answers, like I understand what's going on.

"What about *outside* of school?" I pry further.

"That's where the *secret* part comes in," he smirks.

I think for a minute. "Are you *sure* you don't have a girlfriend?"

He laughs. "I'm *sure.*"

"Then why do we have to be so *secretive?*"

"It'd be...safer. For *you,*" he looks up at me, solemnly.

"What? *Why?*" I feel dread coming on.

"Just...I don't have the best *reputation* around here. I'm sure you've *heard,*" he looks up, raising his eyebrows at me, inquiring.

Does he have surveillance cameras set up in school that recorded mine and Meg's conversation or something?

My face flushes and must look the picture of guilt, because he says, "that's what I thought." He looks down at the table, smiling knowingly. "So, it probably wouldn't be best if you were seen hanging out with me."

He lifts his eyes back up to study my gaze. I'm quiet a minute.

Is that really the reason?

I'm hardly a woman, but I could feel my intuition kicking in. There has to be *another* reason. I'm sure I'll figure it out, though. It can't be too bad, I'm sure.

"Did you fix my bike?" I blurt out.

He fights a smile."You didn't answer my question..."

"Sure, secret agent besties, whatever. Now answer *mine*," I splutter, impatiently.

"Yes, I fixed your bike," he sighs reluctantly.

I fight a smile. Then I think for a minute. "Last question," I say and he rolls his eyes. "Are the rumors I heard about you and your family, actually *true?*" I raise a brow.

He smirks. "Most of them."

Kathey Gray

CHAPTER SIX

It's Complicated

"Okay, spill," Meg demands.

"What?" I ask, distracted, with my face in my locker.

"Don't play stupid with me, you had lunch with Benjamin," she accuses.

I shut my locker. "*Ben*," I correct her.

Her mouth drops open. "Oh-my-gosh...you *like* him."

I shake my head. "We're just friends," I say and start walking.

She grabs my arm and whirls me around, forcing me to face her. "Benjamin doesn't have *friends*," she says emphatically. "He only hangs out with his gang of brothers."

I shrug my shoulders.

She sighs. "Just, be careful okay. I don't *trust* him."

I smile at her. "I'll be fine," I reassure her.

          After school, I ride home on my bike, contemplating. I can't shake this strange feeling that I've started something bad. Like I unknowingly signed up for something dangerous that's going to end up being more than I bargained for. At dinner, I hear my phone buzz. It's a text from Meg. My parents don't even notice as I look down to read it.

Jamie wants to know why you haven't called or texted him.

Before I can respond, she texts me again.

He wants to know if you want to go to the movies with him and me and Aiden this Friday? Unless you have plans with Ben....?

I know she's teasing me, by calling him *Ben* instead of Benjamin. She wants me to say 'no' so she can be right about her assumption of our "relationship". This is a test. I don't think he would want to hang out with me? Besides, he's not my boyfriend or anything, we're just friends...at least that's what *Ben* wants. If that's true though, why do I feel guilty about agreeing to go? She texts me again, impatient as ever.

Well?

Sure, sounds fun. I text back, uncertain.

I don't want to give Jamie the wrong idea. Sure, he's handsome and definitely fun, but I don't really like him like that.

Suddenly, I wish I had Ben's number so I could text him, not that I knew what I'd *say* to him. I didn't know what it was about him, but he seemed different than the other boys in my grade. More serious and intense. Like he carried invisible weights on his shoulders.

Maybe he's not such a terrible guy. Maybe he's just misunderstood?

That night while I'm sleeping, the sound of sirens wakes me up. I sit up in bed, confused. I peek out of my window. I see red and blue lights flashing on the side of Ben's house. Startled, I rise to my feet and go to peek around the corner of my bedroom door. I find that my parent's have been woken up, too and are looking out of the living room windows. I creep tentatively behind them and peek around their heads. There's a police car outside, in front of Ben's house. I gasp and my parents turn around, surprised to find me there.

"Woke you up too, 'eh, buttercup?" My dad asks.

"Yeah," I rub my eyes.

I wonder if Ben is okay?

We watch in silence, as the police come away from Ben's front door with Quinn in their grasp. He has his arms pinned behind him in handcuffs. I cringe as he hurls obscenity after obscenity at the officers.

"Looks like the boys next door are trouble," my dad sighs. "Abby, I want you to stay away from them. You *hear* me?"

I pause and my dad gets irritable.

"*Got it?*" he demands.

"Yes, dad. I got it," I blurt out, hurriedly, already knowing it's an empty promise.

We watch as they load Quinn into the cruiser and drive off. Since the show is over, we all turn and head back to our beds.

"Get some rest, honey." My mom puts her hand on my shoulder, before retiring to her bedroom.

I nod, knowing that will be hard after all that commotion. Also, because of my dad's warning. I guess it works out that Ben wants to be "secret" friends. Now that I know I can't bring him around my parents. Sleep finally finds me though.

The next morning, I wake feeling rougher than usual, after a restless night of sleep. I look at my reflection in the mirror and sigh at how haggard I look today. I go to my parents' bedroom to borrow my mom's concealer to try to hide the dark circles under my eyes. I put on minimal makeup, just mascara, blush and chapstick. I get dressed in a t-shirt and jeans and my Vans. I brush my hair and braid it out of my face. I make myself a bagel with cream cheese for breakfast. Then I put on my parka and backpack and head out. I ride my bike to my usual route, through the alley. I turn the corner and hit my breaks, gasping. Ben is standing in the alley, waiting for me.

"Hey friend, want to walk to school with me?" he calls, grinning.

CHAPTER SEVEN
Secret Friends

Of course I'm surprised to see Ben, especially after what happened last night. He looks *too* good today, like the ultimate bad boy. He's wearing a black leather jacket and rugged, denim jeans. His hair is spiked in a messy disarray. He's smiling mischievously and his eyes twinkle dangerously at me.

"Hi...Ben. I didn't see you, there," I say, breathlessly.

He smiles. "I told you we'd have to be to secretive."

He gestures with his hand for me to come. "Well c'mon, we'll be late."

"Didn't know *you* cared about getting tardies," I quip.

"*I* don't. I was talking about *you*," he smiles.

I force my shaky legs forward and propel towards him. He starts walking beside me.

"*Er—* should I go put my bike back?" I ask, awkwardly, feeling strange that he has to walk next to me.

"No, I'm fine," he smiles shyly.

There is an awkward pause of silence, and the breeze picks up, blowing the scent of his cologne my way. I realize how much I already like him.

"You look tired," he comments.

I flush, in embarrassment.

You look amazing...and smell amazing, I think.

"Did we wake you last night?" he asks and I flush more. He knows what we saw.

"Um...yeah," I admit, knowing he'd probably know if I lied anyway.

"Sorry about that," he smirks, not looking the least bit sorry.

"My dad told me to stay away from you and your brothers," I blurt out, stupidly, mentally cursing myself.

"He *did*, did he?" he smiles wider, entertained with himself. "Smart man," he adds.

"What do *you* think?" he turns to me, suddenly focusing his full attention on me.

I stop riding. "About w-what?" I stammer, nervously.

"Do *you* think you should stay away from me?" he asks, his clear blue eyes watching my response.

I think for a minute, then answer honestly. "I haven't found a reason to yet."

He laughs, and I realize how much I like the sound of it. We turn the corner to the school.

I wonder aloud, "where are your brothers, by the way?"

"Bailing Quinn out of jail," he says simply.

"Why aren't your *parents* doing that?" I scoff.

"My parents are dead," he says, rigidly.

My stomach drops. "*Oh*," I breathe. "I'm sorry, I had no idea," I say, feeling awful and hating the way my voice sounds, bleeding with sympathy.

"You didn't hear *that* rumor, did you?" he asks, resentfully.

"No. No one's told me that," I admit.

"That's because no one *knows*," his mouth sets into a thin line. "We like to keep it that way," he gazes at me, meaningfully.

"Sure. I won't tell anyone," I promise.

"Good," he says, seeming satisfied. "See you in class."

"Okay..." I say, taken aback by his abrupt change in mood.

I watch him as he crosses the yard and walks into the building. I spot Meg in the crowd of students. Her eyes are huge and her mouth is hanging open.

Crap. She saw us.

Her eyes meet with mine, as she starts walking briskly and purposefully towards me, her Auburn hair blowing in the breeze. I avert my eyes, not ready to hear what she has to say. I park my bike and chain it up. She's only a few feet away now. I sigh.

Here we go.

"Ms. Brooks, I do believe you have some *explaining* to do." She smiles hugely, her brown eyes wide with excitement.

After Meg grills me for details all the way from the front lawn to my locker, I'm relieved to get away from her and go to class.

I sit in my seat beside Ben. He doesn't look at me, he just smirks at his desk. At least I think I'm forgiven, for now. We get through class without speaking a word to each other. When the bell rings, I walk out of the classroom. I hear his voice from behind me, as he suddenly grabs my hand, squeezing it and sending a jolt through me.

"*See you at lunch,*" he whispers, in a deep voice.

He releases my hand, just as fast as he grabbed it, blink and you'd miss it. My heart pounds hard in my chest. I turn around, but he's already walking away. He turns and smiles once, before heading down the hall.

Woah...

I like him a lot, this is going to be a problem. But I can't stop smiling.

I can barely concentrate in my next class. I feel like I can barely contain my nerves. When the bell rings, I practically jump out of my seat.

Meg catches up to me. "Are you going to sit with Ben again?" she smiles.

I sigh and smile back. "Maybe"

"Traitor." She punches me in the arm, playfully.

I go through the line and sit at "our" table. Ben joins me a few seconds later. I train my eyes to my food when he first sits down, to keep myself from smiling like an idiot.

"Hi," he smiles when I look up.

"Hi," I smile back.

"Good news, Quinn is out," he smiles, triumphantly.

"That *is* good news," I agree.

Even though, I'm still not sure what he did to get in there?

"Although, I'm sort of glad that he got put in jail in the first place," he smiles crookedly.

My eyebrows knit together and I laugh. "*Why?*"

"Because I got to walk you to school," he winks.

"Oh," I breathe. "Yeah, that was nice." I feel hot all over and at a loss for words, so I blurt out the first thing that comes to mind. "Why *was* he arrested?"

Ben shrugs, looking slightly disappointed. "Who knows"

Suddenly, I see Jamie enter the cafeteria. He scans it, is he looking for *me?* When his eyes land on me, he smiles and waves, heading our way. I feel knots in my stomach forming.

"Who *is* that?" Ben asks, irritably.

"Um, just one of my friends," I mumble, worried.

Jamie reaches our table. "Hey, Abby!"

Behind him, some teachers are headed our way, watching Jamie with disapproval.

"Hey Jamie, what are you doing here?" I try to keep my voice light.

"Well, I had time in between classes and I saw you...and well, since I never really get to *see* you, I wanted to tell you in person..."

Ben's glaring at Jamie, but Jamie refuses to acknowledge him.

"Oh, well what did you want to tell me?" I wonder, curiously.

"That I'm excited about our date on Friday. I'm *so* glad that you agreed to go. Oh, and I'll be picking you up at six, sound good?" he winks.

I nod numbly and force some sort of strange smile at him. The blood drains from my face. I'm too afraid to look over at Ben. Before I can form words, the teachers take Jamie by the arms and start escorting him out of the cafeteria, scolding him as they do. They tell him that juniors aren't allowed in the sophomore lunch. I didn't even know that Jamie *was* a junior. Unaffected, he waves at me and smiles, goofily. I wave back, awkwardly, not wanting to be rude. I look over at Ben and his eyes are blazing. Before I can explain myself, the bell rings. I get up and go to dump my tray, Ben follows me in silence. We walk out of the cafeteria doors and I turn to Ben, his face a composed mask. I'm about to speak, but he does first.

"Is he your boyfriend?" he asks, his eyes wide with curiosity.

"No, Ben. I told you we're just *friends*. We're just going on a double date with Meg and Aiden, that's all," I explain.

"He *wants* to be," he says, like it's a known fact.

I shake my head. "It's not like that, we don't talk. He doesn't even have my number."

"I don't have your number either," he points out, his playful demeanor resurfacing again.

I pause. "Are you asking me for my number?" I feel the corners of my mouth lifting, slightly.

"Depends on if you'll give it to me," he smiles, mischievously.

"Give me your phone," I roll my eyes, smiling.

CHAPTER EIGHT

Superstitions

I have to ride my bike home by myself after school because Ben's brothers came to pick him up. Not that I really care, but it was nice to have his company. It's foggy and already starting to drizzle, so I ride home fast. I lean my bike against the wall and unlock the door with my house key. I toss my backpack on the floor and stick my head into the fridge, looking for something to eat. I hear my phone ringing and go to check it. It's a Face-Time call from Riley! I can't believe I haven't talked to her since before school started! It's been weeks! I hope she's not furious with me. I swipe the screen to "accept" and wait for the screaming to start.

But then I surprise myself and beat her to it. "*Riley!*" I shout, excited as her face materializes onto the screen.

"Hey Abbs! Oh my gosh! It's really *you!* I need to talk to you *so* bad!" She jumps up and down in her seat.

"Yes it's me!" I laugh. "What do you need to talk to me about?"

"We have a new student at school, his name is Chad and he's *soooo* cute!"

"Really? That's weird, we never used to get new students," I muse.

"I know, right? Especially *cute* ones!" she says, bouncing in her seat.

"Good to hear that you don't miss me too much," I say bitterly.

"What are you talking about? I miss you to the moon and back!" She opens her skinny arms to show me how much, her short black bob shaking.

I laugh again. "I miss you too."

"So how do you like it there? What's it like at school?"

"Just like any other school I guess, a lot bigger though. No one even knows I *exist*, pretty much," I laugh. "But I have made a few new friends." She raises an eyebrow. "But there's no one like *you* here of course. No one could ever take *your* place," I smile sweetly at her. She nods her head and smiles, satisfied. "There is this guy..." I start.

Her eyes grow wide and she smiles, widely. "I'm all ears."

After a long talk with Riley, who of course encourages me to have a hot, heated affair with Ben, I go back to my routine. I do my homework and wait for my parents to get home. I hear my phone buzz, and look down at it.

Hi.

It's from an unknown number. It's *Ben?!?*

I text back. *Who is this?*

A friend.

Really? It *has* to be Ben.

Is this friend in my Algebra class? I message him.

Yes.

My heart skips.

What are you doing? He writes.

Well, I was just talking about you.

Nothing. I lie. I really *should* finish my homework...

Want to go for a walk?

Alone with Ben again?

Sure. I answer.

I'll be there in a minute.

My heart leaps in my throat.

He's coming over!

I look at the time. I only have an hour until my parents get home! I leap off of my bed.

Homework can wait!

I run to the bathroom and take my frizzy braid out. I change out of my wrinkled shirt, spray some perfume on, and trade my Vans for my boots. I hear a knock at the door and walk nervously to it. Scout runs to it and starts barking.

"Scout, *shh!*" I pull her back.

I open the door to find Ben standing there, smiling crookedly with mischief in his eyes. Scout growls at my side. I shush her again, before pushing her back into the house, shutting and locking the door.

"She's a good judge of character," he smiles, entertained.

What's that supposed to mean?

"Ready?" he grins.

"Yeah," I smile back, shyly. "I only have an hour," I inform him.

"Well, that's not much time for fun," he beams.

My breath gets caught in my throat, I suddenly worry about his intentions. My face must show my concern because he laughs. "We'll take the shorter trail then," he decides.

"*Trail?*" I squeak. "Like in the woods?"

"Yeah, they're right around the corner from here," he smiles.

I still haven't gotten over his accent, I hold back the swoon that threatens to break free every time he speaks. He holds his hand out to me and I take it, hesitantly. I know that we're supposed to be *friends*, but this is seeming more like a date by the minute. We walk away from our houses, hand in hand. I keep peeking up at him, making sure this is all real. We turn the corner and sure enough there is a park, with trails leading into the forest. We approach the trail. I stare up at the dark, ominous trees and he senses my nervousness.

"It's okay, we'll stay close." He squeezes my hand. "The sun will be going down in about an hour and we don't want to be out here when it *does*."

I look at him, alarmed, and he laughs. "It's okay, I'll protect you," he smiles, warmly.

I flush and look away. He leads me into the woods and up a short trail. We sit at a small campsite. I'm relieved that I can still see the park through the trees from where we are. We're not very far at all.

"It's beautiful here," I say, looking up at the trees.

"Yes it is," he says, staring at me instead of the trees.

"Do you like it here?" he asks.

"Yes."

"Where did you live before?" he asks, curiously.

"Minnesota."

"What's it like there?" He continues his questioning.

"Um," I laugh. "There's a lot of farms."

He laughs. "Sounds like fun."

"Not really," I admit.

"Have *you* always lived here?" I turn the questions on him. His voice is much less boring to listen to than mine.

"No," he leans back a little, instantly uncomfortable.

"I didn't think so," I smile.

"Oh, *really?* Why not?" he smirks, knowingly.

"Because of your accent."

He pauses, before speaking carefully. "I was born in Ireland, we moved to the states when I was eight."

"Why?" I pick up a stick and twist it in my hands.

"That was after my parents died, after the fire. We came to live with our aunt," he watches my hands, eyes downcast.

"*Fire?*" I stop twirling the stick.

"Our house caught on fire. Me and my brothers ran out...our parents didn't make it." He looks away, watching a bird flying into a tree. It's silent a moment, as I come to terms with the fact that the life he's lived, is something I can't fathom.

"I can't imagine, you must've went through a lot." I try to keep my voice even, void of empathy. I don't want to upset him.

He shrugs. "I'm a Blake, we're built to withstand hardship." I nod. "The weird part is," he continues suddenly, "when the police investigated the fire, they couldn't tell where it started. People said it was the curse."

"*Curse?*" My stomach sinks.

He looks up at me, his eyes wide and serious. "The Blake curse."

I sit, staring at him, waiting to see if he's joking. But he's stone-faced.

"You *believe* in it," I say, stating the words, rather than asking.

"*Yes,*" he says, emphatically.

I pause. "So...what's the curse?" I pry further, even though I'm afraid to hear the answer.

His lips set in a thin line and he seems to contemplate for a moment, before answering. "I don't know for sure," he shrugs, suddenly indifferent. "It's more like a superstition, urban legend, kind of thing." He looks up at the sky. "We should go, it's getting dark.."

I'm taken aback by his sudden diversion, but when I look up at the sky to see that he's right. I look at my phone.

It's six-thirty!

I leap up. "My parents will be home soon!"

He laughs and gets up too, taking my hand in his. A tingly, warm feeling runs through my body.

"This was nice, you know. Besides the, uh, creepy parts," I say.

He walks beside me, smiling. "It *is* nice." The way he looks at me gives me butterflies in my stomach.

We get to my house and he walks me up to my front door. There's a sudden tension that wasn't there before, it makes my stomach flip.

"Well, see you later, I guess." I fumble with my key, awkwardly.

He walks up to me and stands within inches of my face. My breath hitches, as I anticipate the possibility of him trying to kiss me. He reaches up, his blue eyes intense, and brushes his hand through my hair. He pulls out a piece of a leaf.

"You had a leaf in your hair," he says, his voice husky.

"*Oh*," I breathe. Disappointment floods me.

"See you later," he says, starting to walk away.

"Okay," I say, defeated. I turn and start to open the door. I slip inside and go to shut it, but stop when I hear Ben call my name.

"Abby," he calls.

I poke my head back out. "Yes?"

He's still standing on my porch. "Think of me tomorrow. You know, on your *date*," he winks.

What a strange thing to say.

I flush wildly. "I will," I smirk.

CHAPTER NINE

Date Night

Luckily for me, my parents got home *after* Ben had left. I went back to finishing my homework. As I laid in bed that night, I couldn't stop thinking about everything Ben had said. How he believed his family was under some sort of curse, and how he had lost his parents when he was only eight years old. The more I got to know Ben, the more I *wanted* to know. He was unlike anyone I'd ever met. But I also couldn't shake the underlying fear that it wasn't *safe* for me to be sneaking around with him. He had said it himself, that the rumors are mostly true about him. He was *admitting* he was trouble.

Was that the most intriguing part about him? Or was I just a sucker for an Irish accent?

Whatever it was, I was certain of one thing, I couldn't get him off of my mind. It was a waste of time deliberating about it anyway. The way I felt when I thought he was going to kiss me, was proof enough. I couldn't stay away even if I *wanted* to. Sleep finally found me when I accepted that.

The next morning, I woke up late and had to rush to school without breakfast. I was tardy to my first class. All day, I couldn't wait for lunch to come so I could sit with Ben. But when it did, he wasn't there. I sullenly went to go sit with Meg.

"Your boyfriend's absent today?" She asked, looking down and stabbing a green bean on her tray.

"He's not my boyfriend," I mutter, automatically. Instead of arguing with me, she just gives me a look.

"Anyway," she changes the subject. "I'm so excited for our double date tonight! I've been wanting to see 'He Loves Me' since I saw the preview!"

I crinkle my nose. "*That's* what we're seeing?"

"*Yes! Oh my gosh!* Can you at least *pretend* to be excited?" She slaps her hands on her knees, exasperated.

"Sorry," I smile. "I *am* excited about hanging out with you," I say sweetly.

"Good enough for me," she laughs.

After school, I ride home nervously. I can't believe I agreed to do this. I didn't think Jamie would be picking me up by himself *and* I'd be riding in the car *alone* with him.

Meg has been blowing up my phone since I got home. I made sure to dress carefully, I didn't want to give Jamie the wrong impression, but I don't want to look like I just don't care either. I finally settle for a dressy blue top, jeans and my boots. I put on a little makeup and curl my hair. I look in the mirror at my reflection and wipe a little of the makeup off. I grab my parka, just in case. I hear a honk outside and shake my head, in disbelief.

He can't get out of his car to knock at the door?

I open the door and whirl around, ready to give Jamie a piece of my mind, but I stop short, shocked at the sight of his vehicle. It's some sort of shiny, flashy car. I have no idea what kind, but I know it's expensive.

If he drives that then why would he ever hitch a ride? I wonder.

I turn back around, shutting and locking the door swiftly. I approach the car with my eyes wide. I'm about to compliment his ride, when I hear Jamie let out a low whistle.

"Hey baby!" he yells.

My mouth pops open for a brief moment, but I recover quickly. Jamie sure wasn't *shy*. It would be easier to be mad at him if he wasn't so damn goofy and charming. He gets out of the car and I'd be lying if I said he didn't look attractive. He's wearing fitted jeans and white low v-neck t-shirt that hugs his muscles. His curly hair is even messier than usual and his vibrant, green eyes are hidden behind aviator sunglasses. He walks around to the passenger door and holds it open for me.

Oh, now he wants to be a gentleman?

"You, look gorgeous," he grins widely.

"Thanks," I flush.

I get in and inhale the scent of new car. Jamie closes the door and walks around to his side and gets in, shutting his door.

"Nice car, is it yours?" I smirk.

"Yes and thank you. It suits me well," he beams.

"What is it?" I ask, curiously, attempting to make small-talk.

"It's an Aston Martin Vantage."

I nod. "I don't know how much about cars, but it's beautiful," I admit.

He looks over at me. "I only like beautiful things."

I blush and look at my hands.

"Ready for our date?" he asks, excitedly.

"Yup," I smile and he laughs.

He puts the car in reverse and we're on our way. Portland is huge and has a ton of things to do. I watch the malls, businesses and restaurant after restaurant pass by, as we drive through the heart of the city. I remain mostly silent as we drive, listening to the songs on the radio. We finally pull up to a huge theater and park. I see Meg and Aiden pull up in his truck. She waves enthusiastically. Jamie hops out of the car and I realize I should probably stay put because he's attempting to be a gentleman. In the moment it takes him to make his way over to my door, my phone buzzes in my lap. I pick it up and swipe the screen.

Hi.

It's Ben.

Just then Jamie opens the door and holds his hand out to me. "Shall we? M'lady?"

I click off of the message and stick the phone in my small, cross-body purse. I let him take my hand, noticing the difference from the feeling of his hand in mine, to Ben's. I didn't feel tingly when Jamie held my hand. Luckily, Meg saves me by running up and hugging me, forcing Jamie to let go of my hand.

"You look hot," she raves.

I wave her comment away nonchalantly. "You look hotter."

She giggles and twirls for me. She decided to dress to the nines, in a short dress and heels.

"Alright, alright, you *both* look hot. Can we go see the movie now?" Aiden complains, with a slight smile on his face.

"You checking out my date, bro?" Jamie jokes.

Of course that makes us all laugh. We walk up and buy our tickets and go get our snacks. While we're in line, my phone buzzes inside my purse, it momentarily distracts me.

"Abby?" Jamie calls my attention.

"Yes?"

"I said do you want candy, too?" He waits, expectantly.

"Oh, yes! Peanut M&M's," I smile.

"Good choice," he smiles back.

We go to sit down in our seats. While everyone is getting adjusted, I pull out my phone to check it. I keep it down and to the side of me, so no one will see it. It's another text from Ben.

Is he doing this on purpose?

Missed eating lunch with you today. It reads.

Before I can process what he's wrote, Jamie throws his arm around my shoulders. I immediately put the phone down, sliding it under my leg. I try to contain my surprise as Jamie smiles down at me. I force a smile back. Meg is watching us, smiling nervously. Her eyes scan my face, silently asking, *is that okay?* When Jamie looks toward the screen, I widen my eyes at her to convey that I'm uncomfortable. Reading my signal, she helps me out.

"Abby, come with me to the bathroom?" She stares.

"Okay," I agree.

Jamie slides his arm off of me and starts talking to Aiden about a basketball game. Once we're in the bathroom, she giggles.

"Sorry, Jamie seems to come on kind of strong, huh?"

"Yeah," I laugh. Then I raise my eyebrows at her. "He called me 'baby' earlier."

Her eyebrows shoot up. *"What?* Oh my gosh! He's crazy!" She bursts into a fit of laughter.

"Yeah, he sure doesn't lack confidence," I snort. "Or *money*," I add.

"Yeah, he's *loaded*," she agrees. *"And* a hunk," she adds, hopeful.

"Yeah...but," I start.

The rest of the sentence, that I stopped myself from saying, hangs in the air.

There's a pause and the bathroom is silent a moment. "But he's not *Ben?*" she guesses.

I smile, apologetically.

Despite all the moves Jamie tries to put on me, and the horrendously over-done, way too predictable storyline of the movie, I still manage to have a good time. I haven't texted Ben back yet, but I'm sure he knows what I'm doing. The ride back with Jamie is more awkward than the ride to the movies. There's a lingering feeling of expectation hanging between us. I had that same feeling with

Ben yesterday, but it was mixed with excitement. This time I'm hoping that Jamie *won't* try to kiss me.

We pull up in my driveway, parking behind my parent's truck. I see a flash of something coming from Ben's front porch. Before I can look to see what it is, Jamie speaks up.

"You sure know how to show a guy a good time," he jokes.

I laugh, nervously, my eyes involuntarily trailing to where I saw the flash. I notice that there's a small glowing light, something's lit up. The end of a cigarette?

"I had fun, too. Thanks for taking me," I smile, politely.

Jamie looks smitten.

Uh-oh.

He leans a little closer, his face inches from mine. I can't stop focusing on that light, though. All of a sudden, a car passes behind us, flashing its headlights across mine and Ben's houses. I spot Ben, shirtless, lounging on a chair on his front porch.

Is he *smoking?*

I must make a face because Jamie follows my eyes.

"Why is that creep staring at us?" he says, annoyed.

I swallow, nervously. "I don't know. He's probably just waiting for one of his brothers to get home." I attempt to shrug off Ben's strange behavior.

I take his moment of distraction as my ticket to get out his car. "I'd better go, thanks Jamie!" I smile and squeeze his hand for a quick second.

He looks wounded momentarily, before resuming to his cocky grin. "Later babe," he winks.

I hop out of his car and wave. He backs out and drives away. I stand there in the driveway for a moment, wondering if Ben will acknowledge me. But he just sits there, stone-faced and in the dark. His face only illuminated by the light of his cigarette, as he remains smoking and watching me.

"Goodnight, Ben!" I yell, and walk inside.

CHAPTER TEN
The Kiss

When I got home last night, I had to answer all of my mom's embarrassing questions about my first "date". I had to pretend that I was excited about it. If my mom knew who I was *really* interested in, she probably wouldn't have felt so damn skippy about it. I slept in late that morning, for some reason, exhausted for some reason. I heard my mom's voice calling me from the kitchen.

"*Abby, I made eggs and bacon!*" She yelled.

I rolled around in my bed and rubbed the sleep out of my eyes. Then I opened my curtains, curious to see what the day looked like outside, wondering if it was going to rain or not. But I'm stunned when I find a single red rose sitting on the outside of my window sill. I watch as rain drops start sprinkling on its petals. I looked up at the sky, realizing it's going to be another rainy day. Lifting the old latch on the window, I unlocked it. It's rusted and old, so it takes some effort to slide it upward. I reach my hand out of the screenless window and pick up the wet rose. Raising it to my nose, I inhale the fresh aroma. My mom yells my name again, and I flinch, startled and prick my finger on one of its thorns.

"*Ow*," I complain, as I see the bead of blood forming on the tip of my finger.

"*Coming!*" I yell back, annoyed.

I decide to hide the rose under my bed, sticking its stem into one of my books and closing it. I get a band-aid from my bathroom and wrap it around my finger. Then I slide my window shut again and lock it. My intuition tells me that the rose is from Ben, Jamie's too unoriginal. The thought makes a huge grin spread across my face. I also know that if I ask Ben about it, he'll probably deny it. I actually giggle when I come to that realization.

I eat breakfast with my parents, then take a bath. Later on, as I'm lying in my bed, reading, my mom comes in, looking dressed up.

"You look *nice*, mom," I comment, arching a brow at her, suspiciously.

"Oh, thank you!" She flushes, smoothing her dress. "Me and your dad are going on a date!" She smiles.

"You *are?*" I ask, incredulous.

"*Yes!* We're not too *old* to go on dates!" She puts her hand on her hip, pursing her lips.

I laugh. "I never said *that!*"

She grows serious. "That is, if you feel *okay* to be alone for a few hours?"

I roll my eyes. "Mom, I'm *sixteen*, I'm not a baby. Besides, I have a cell phone...and Scout," I smile. Scout walks in, as if on cue, wagging her big tail.

"Okay," she sighs. "We're going to lunch and a movie. I already made you a sandwich in the fridge," she informs me.

"Okay, thanks mom. Have fun," I smile, my heart already racing.

"Love you, honey." She walks over and kisses me on the forehead.

"Love you, too," I say, silently wishing that she'd hurry up and leave already.

She walks out of my room and closes the door. I wait to hear the sound of the truck driving away.

I pick up my phone and text Ben. *Want to hang out?*

I'm disappointed when he doesn't answer me. An hour passes, before I decide to try his house. I get dressed and wind my hair up into a bun. I put on a little mascara and blush, just in case. Even though, he might not even be home. When I go to leave, Scout whines by my side.

"It's okay, girl. I'll be right back." I pat her head. I shut the door and lock it.

I walk over to Ben's house, nervously. Up close, his house is kind of creepy. It's made of dark wood and the windows are covered with black curtains. I walk up the front porch steps and tentatively knock on the door. I hear loud, banging footsteps approaching the door and the sound of a male's voice cursing. I start to regret coming, I contemplate turning around and running back to my house, but it's too late. The door creaks open and one of Ben's brothers steps out, I think his name is Joseph. He towers over me, regarding me with a detached expression. I can't help but notice how much different he looks than Ben. His black hair is curly and stands out against his pale skin. His dark blue eyes scrutinize me.

"We don't want any *Girl Scout* cookies," he drawls, in a heavy Irish accent.

"I'm not a Girl Scout," I respond, with more attitude than I meant to. "I'm looking for *Ben?*" I inform him.

"*Who?*" he asks, pulling a cigarette out of his pocket and lighting it.

I raise my eyebrows. "*Ben*, you know, your *brother?*"

He pauses a moment, taking a long, slow drag, keeping me waiting. He blows the smoke in my face. "Oh, him. He isn't here," he says finally.

I cough and wave it away. *What a jerk!* It also hasn't gone unnoticed by me, that most of the brothers smoke and are underage.

"Can you tell him that Abby came by?" I ask, hopelessly.

"Sure thing, Amber," he replies, then turns and walks back through the door, shutting it behind him.

I sigh. I doubt Ben is going to get *that* message. I decide to walk to the park around the corner. It's only one o' clock in the afternoon after all, and the rain has slowed to a sprinkle. I pull up my hood and make my way there. I arrive at the park and note how it's always eerily empty here. I follow the same trail that Ben and I took, sitting in the same spot we did last time. I get bored quickly though, without Ben. I still have a lot of time to kill before my parents get home, so I decide to take another trail, that winds further into the woods. The smell of fresh air mixed with rain and the trees invites my senses, luring me in. I inhale it, deeply. Suddenly, I hear the sound of a stick breaking. I turn to see what it is, and trip over the raised root of a tree. The klutz I am, I twist my ankle.

"*Owwww*," I wince, hopping for a moment.

"Haven't you *heard?* Girls aren't supposed to wander in the woods alone," I hear an all too familiar voice say.

I turn around and Ben is standing a few feet behind me, smirking, clearly entertained. He's wearing an army green jacket, jeans and black Converse. He has on a black baseball cap, on backwards, making him look boyishly cute.

"How'd you know I was out here?" I pretend to be creeped, but I actually couldn't be more thrilled and relieved that he showed up.

"*Well*," he says, smiling warmly. "When my brother said a girl came by looking for me, I figured it was you. I knocked on your door, but no one was home," he continues. "I figured I'd look here just in case, and look I found *you!*" he gestures his hand at me, smiling. "Although, I didn't expect you to be so *far* in the woods," he grimaces. "Especially since you seemed so nervous the last time we were here," he scratches the back of his neck.

For some reason, I feel like I'm being scolded and feel the need to explain myself. "...Well, I just wanted to explore a little," I explain, slowly sitting down. "I might've twisted my ankle though."

I pull up my jeans and notice that it's swollen and red. I sigh.

"That looks to be true," he agrees, looking down at it.

"I don't know if I can make it home by myself," I admit.

"I figured that much," he smirks.

He walks over to me and holds out his hand to me. I put my hand in his and he pulls me up. He picks up my arm and drapes it over his shoulders. I can feel his hard muscles through his jacket and gulp. I'm so close that I can smell his woodsy cologne. I try to focus on walking, or limping.

"Let's get you home, lost girl," he smiles.

"Thank you, I'm *so* glad you showed up," I breathe.

"Maybe I *shouldn't* have," he laughs. "If it wasn't for me coming, this wouldn't have happened to you," he points out.

I realize that what he's saying is actually true. I tripped over that root when I heard him approach. But I also know, that I could've heard *any* noise and the same thing would've probably happened to me, *and* no one would've been around to help me.

"I'm glad you showed up," I smile. "And I probably would've gotten hurt on my own anyway," I admit. "I'm not the most graceful person around." My cheeks burn.

"Oh, I doubt that," he encourages me.

"Stay around me long enough and you'll find out," I raise my eyebrows at him.

"I just might have to then," he winks at me. My insides feel like they melt from the gesture.

The terrain is harder to maneuver while limping. I constantly trip and have onto clutch Ben's shoulders to keep from falling. Until I actually *do* fall. I end up pulling Ben down with me. He lands on top of me. We both laugh at first, but the atmosphere changes. The air becomes heavy. My heartbeat pounds in my chest, slowly.

Ben's smile melts away and his eyes scan my face. "You're beautiful, Abby," he says, softly. His fingers graze my cheek. I begin to question if this is really happening, or if I'm dreaming. Whichever the answer, I knew what was going to happen next. My stomach flips.

He closes the space between us, pressing his lips to mine. His kiss is soft and slow, I feel like my body is melting underneath his. Time seems to stop and I close my eyes, letting the odd sensation that my body is floating, take over. If it wasn't for the feel of the damp leaves under my back, I fear I would've floated away. Sensations that I wasn't aware of, awaken. But the blissful moment is over all too soon. Ben pulls back abruptly, looking alarmed.

"What's wrong?" I panic.

"I'm so sorry, I *shouldn't* have done that," he pales.

"It was just a kiss, well, an *amazing* one. But I *wanted* you to," I try to reassure him.

"That's part of the *problem*." He puts his hands on his knees, looking away, troubled.

I stare at him, bemused. He holds his hand out to me and I take it, reluctantly. He pulls me up and helps me brush the wet bracken off of my now damp clothes. We resume our position and proceed to make our way back toward our houses. He stays silent a while, until we get onto our street. I can feel the tension radiating off of his shoulders. I decide to break the silence first.

"Why were you watching me last night?" I ask.

He looks away. "I wasn't."

"But you looked right at me," I argue.

"I was having a smoke, Abby, it's no big deal," he mutters, irritated.

"You don't like me going on dates with Jamie?" I pry, answering for him.

I notice him flinch slightly when I mention Jamie's name, but he keeps walking, ignoring me. I grow impatient.

"You *can't do that*, it's not *fair*," I say, fervently.

"Do *what?*" He looks anywhere but at me.

"Act like it doesn't bother you when you see me with Jamie, when it *does*. Or, even better, tell me that we're just "friends" and then *kiss* me!" My voice starts to climb.

He sighs and grits down on his teeth.

"Well? *Say something,* Ben! You're so *confusing!* Do you *like me* or *not?*" My voice trembles with anticipation and frustration.

He stops walking, abruptly and turns me to face him, holding me in his arms.

"Yes! Yes, I like you, Abby! Okay? I think about you *all the time!* Is *that* what you wanted to *hear?*" His sincere voice is laced with worry.

"*You do?*" I whisper, breathless.

He nods, closing his eyes briefly in defeat.

"*How much?*" My voice comes out, nearly inaudible. But he hears me.

"*Too much*," he whispers back.

CHAPTER ELEVEN

Wounded

After Ben's confession, he looked even *more* mortified than he did after he kissed me. He insisted on not discussing it further. He helped me to my front door and told me that he'd see me at school. I swear I couldn't keep up with his hot to cold mood changes. My parents came home about a half an hour later and found me icing my ankle while lying on my bed, reading. Scout was laying on the floor, beside my bed.

"What *happened?*" My mom asked, appalled, when she walked in.

Luckily, I already had a lie ready. "I tripped over Scout, I didn't know she was lying outside of the bathroom door."

"*Oh!*" My mom said, concerned. "Are you alright?"

"Um, I think I sprained it," I admitted, reluctantly.

Just then my dad walked in. "What's up, baby girl?"

He looked down at my ankle. "*Ohhhh*, yep, that's definitely sprained," he grimaces.

"*Ugh*," I complain.

"Stay in bed tomorrow, doctor's orders," he points at me.

"Yes," my mom encourages. "Luckily, *I'll* be home to take care of you," she smiles.

Great. Twenty-four hour surveillance, I think.

"Did you have fun on your date?" I ask my mom, relieved to change the subject.

"Oh yes, we went to this great seafood restaurant," she starts.

She continues to describe every detail of the restaurant, menu, food and dessert. Then she starts telling me about the sad movie they saw. My dad has already left the room, and my eyes have started to glaze over. My mind drifts to thoughts of Ben. His smile, his laugh, his eyes....

"*Abby,*" my mom calls my attention.

"Huh?" I say.

"I *said*, do you think you can get a ride to school from Meghan or Jamie this week?" she repeats, in a slightly irritated tone. It doesn't go unnoticed by me, how she tries to play it cool when she says *Jamie's* name, but fails completely.

"Oh...yeah," I nod.

"Okay, good. Well I'm going to go change, do you need anything?" she asks, glancing over her shoulder.

"No, I'm fine mom," I answer.

"Okay, I'll be back in a few minutes," she reassures me.

She leaves the room and I mutter to myself, "*I was worried about that.*"

A few minutes later, I hear her call from the kitchen. "*Abby! Why didn't you eat your sandwich?*"

Oops. Guess I forgot to eat lunch. My stomach growls.

That night, while I lie in bed, tossing and turning, I hear a loud commotion. It sounds like it's coming from Ben's house. I stop fidgeting and lie still, listening quietly. I hear a loud bang and my heart beats fast. I can hear Ben and his brother arguing, loudly.

"*I can't believe you saw her again!*" A voice scolds.

I can't hear if Ben responds. It's silent a moment, so I assume he *did* say something.

"*So you think that the rules don't apply to you?*" His brother asks, in a condescending tone. "*You think you're the exception?*" He chuckles, darkly. Another pause. "*I don't care if she hears! She needs to hear this!*" The voice thunders.

I feel myself shrink down in my bed. He *wants* me to hear them argue? I hope they don't try to come over *here* next!

"*You're putting her in danger and you're putting us in danger! We can't afford for you to do that!*" His brother yells.

I finally hear Ben's voice surface from the chaos. "*It's not a big deal, it's not that serious,*" he says, calmly. "*Calm down.*"

Ben's brother lowers his voice, but I can still make out what he says. "*This is your last warning,*" he threatens.

Kathey Gray

"Yeah, I get it. Stop acting like you're my dad," Ben says, annoyed.

"We all know why I have to. We all know why he isn't here. This is the whole point of the rules," he pleads with Ben.

Ben mumbles something unintelligible and it seems like the argument is over. This is the *second* time I've overheard a heated argument, about *me*.

I start to get the feeling that Ben and I will *never* get a real chance. His brothers won't *allow* it for some reason. Maybe it really *was* against their religion? But from what Meg told me, Ben was *far* from a virgin. I don't understand *what* their problem is with me. Why am *I* different from those two skanks I saw him with at lunch the other day? I start to think about the way Ben reacted after he kissed me, how he said he *shouldn't* have. He seemed...*afraid*.

What the *hell* would scare Benjamin Blake?

He reacted the same way after he admitted that he liked me. Like it was *wrong*. Then again, he was there for me when I flew off of my bike *and* he helped me home. He fixed my bike tire. He leaves me roses. He always shows up whenever I need help. It's mind boggling. He's beckoning me to him and pushing me away at the same time. A sick feeling of dread settles into my stomach spreads through me. This wasn't some kind of morbid game he was

86

playing with me, was it? I sigh to myself, it would've been so much easier if I *had* just liked someone like Jamie...but it wouldn't be half as interesting.

The next day, my mom is waiting on me hand and foot. It's strangely pleasant. She walks in with a tray of food, like I'm a medical patient in the hospital.

"Breakfast," she smiles.

My mouth waters at the sight of the blueberry pancakes she's made.

"Aw, mom, you're so sweet. Thank you," I smile, sitting up in my bed.

"No problem," she says, pleased with herself.

She leans down to hand me the tray. I reach over to take it from her, but accidentally knock the fork off of the plate, in my still tired state. It clinks onto the floor, landing under my bed.

"*Oops!*" I exclaim, automatically trying to reach for it.

"I got it," my mom says, hurriedly, squatting to her knees to retrieve it.

In my horror, I remember the rose under my bed. But it's too late, she finds it anyway.

"Abby— *what's this?*" She picks up the book and opens it, revealing the red rose. She stands up, scrutinizing my face.

"That's, um, Jamie gave it to me," I stutter, embarrassed.

"Then why'd you *hide* it under your bed?" She raises her eyebrows at me.

I shrug. "I forgot about it."

Her lips turn down in a slight grimace. "Well, it's *lovely*," she perks up, smiling. "It should be in a vase," she shoots me a scolding look.

She holds up her finger and sets the book down on my bed. She leaves the room, taking the rose with her. When she returns, she's holding a glass vase with water containing the single red rose. She leans over me and sets it in my window sill.

"There, much better," she says, putting her hands on her hips and nodding.

I smile weakly, unsure of this whole charade.

"Enjoy your breakfast." She turns on her heel and leaves the room, closing the door behind her.

The rest of the day continues that way. My mom brings me lunch and insists on helping me to and from the bathtub when I bathe. She brings me dinner and tucks me in for the night. I finish my book and turn on the small TV my parents got for me the other day. Scout walks in, wagging her big, furry tail. She hops in the bed with me.

"Hey girl," I smile and hold my hand out to pet her. "Sorry, I had to blame this all on *you*," I whisper to her conspiratorially. "When I get better, I'll take you for a long walk to make up for it, *okay?*"

She wags her tail to signal that she likes that idea. We snuggle up until I fall asleep.

The next morning, I text Meg to make sure she's still coming. I had made arrangements last night for her to come get me.

Hey, you can still give me a ride to school, right? I text her.

She texts me back. *OMG I totally forgot! Aiden picked me up and we're at Mc. Donald's already.*

I panic. *Crap! How am I going to get to school?*

A moment later, Meg texts me again. *I texted Jamie for you.He's coming to get you.*

What?????

I can't *believe* she texted him.

Oh, well, I guess it's better than limping there, I think.

I limp to the kitchen to make myself some toast. A few minutes later, I hear a knock at the door, and limp over to answer it. I open it, and Scout runs over and sniffs at Jamie. She wags her tail. Jamie reaches down to pet her and she licks his hand.

Hmmm, I think, *that is certainly not how she greeted Ben when she met him.*

"Hey girl," he coos, in a friendly tone.

"How'd you *know* she was a girl?" I ask.

"Wild guess," he smirks. "Ladies *love* me."

I roll my eyes.

"So, I heard there was a damsel in distress that needed my assistance?" His eyes examine my wrapped ankle, follow up my body and land on my face. My cheeks heat from the action.

"Thanks for coming, Jamie," I smile.

"*Anytime*," he winks at me.

He walks up to me and wraps my arm around his shoulders. Then he wraps his free arm around my waist, causing me to gasp at the unexpected contact.

Jamie helps me out of the door and to his car. When we get to school, he helps me as I limp through the parking lot. I have a strange premonition that I'm being watched, and look up to scan my surroundings. My eyes land on Ben and his brothers, getting out of their SUV. Ben is staring at us, his eyes piercing through the distance like a sharp arrow. His expression is livid. The set of his jaw is rigid and his stance is tense and hostile. Ben's oldest brother, Max, notices and lightly punches Ben on the arm to get his attention. He nods at Ben to follow them and Ben reluctantly does.

Jamie follows my gaze. "C'mon, Abby," he says softly.

The day is increasingly awkward, as Jamie and Meg take turns escorting me to classes. Ben ignores me in Algebra II, and we have a test that I do horribly on. If it wasn't for it being mine and Ben's only class together, I would've switched it a long time ago. Things are even *worse* at lunch. I spot Ben sitting alone again and start to hobble my way over to him. His eyes meet mine and he shakes his head 'no' at me, in warning.

Wounded, emotionally and physically, I go sit with Meg. Things are so strange and tense between me and Ben. I don't know *what's* going on anymore.

Jamie gives me a ride home after school. I thank him again. Although, I am grateful to him, I hate having to depend on people. I can't wait for my ankle to heal. I think Jamie hopes for the *opposite*. When I think about the way Ben looked at me today and the way he's been acting, it makes my heart sink.

As I sit on my bed, doing my homework. I open my curtains to let the sunlight in. I can't believe it's actually shining today. Too bad it doesn't lighten my mood though. I'm surprised when I see that Ben's curtains are also open. I can see him sitting at a desk in his room, typing something on his laptop. Almost as if he can sense me watching, he turns his head and glances my way. My heart stops at the cold look he gives me. He stands up and closes the curtains, yanking them roughly into place. I sigh deeply, disheartened. My eyes drift to the rose in the window sill, still looking as fresh and fragrant as the day I found it. I look back to Ben's window, finding it ironic, how he's so close, but so far.

CHAPTER TWELVE
Fair Warning

The rest of the week seems to follow the same routine. My foot is better by Wednesday, so I start to ride my bike to school again. Jamie offers to take me to school from now on, insisting that it wouldn't be any trouble to him, but I politely decline. Things with Ben have reached an all time low. He doesn't even look my way anymore. He won't speak to me. It's like we never met. It's heartbreaking, but I can't change it. I've been calling Riley on Face-Time almost every night, it's cheered me up some. *Her* love life has taken off, incidentally. She's now dating the new, cute boy at school, Chad. I figure I can live vicariously through her for a while.

I decide to take Scout for a walk, since it's Friday and I have no other plans. Besides, I did promise her one when I got better. Scout is overjoyed to be out of the house for a while, she wags her big fluffy tail, happily. We walk down the alley for a while, staying out of sight. The ground is wet and smells of rain. I inhale the fresh scent deeply. It's an overcast day, my new favorite. I'm completely at ease and relaxed, and I close my eyes for a moment, reveling. When I open them, I'm stunned to see three dark figures walking towards me. They're laughing and joking until they notice me. Beside me, Scout starts growling. I recognize who they all are now. All of the Blake brothers, *minus Ben*. I turn and quickly start walking the other way, pulling Scout by the leash.

"*Hey!*" I hear one of them call.

"*Hey Amber, come back! We want to have a word with 'ya!*"

Scout barks at them, before I pull her away and start jogging with her.

"*Slow down!*" They laugh. "*We just want to talk with 'ya!*"

But somehow, they've already caught up with me. I hear one of their voices right behind me.

"*Abigail,*" one of them says, catching me by the arm, halting me.

I turn around, knowing that I can't outrun them anyway. Scout barks furiously and lunges at Quinn, the one who grabbed my arm. She bites his leg, latching down on his jeans.

"Ow, *shit!*" he exclaims, letting go of me and jumping back.

Scout barks at him, ferociously, baring her fangs.

"Cute dog," Joseph smirks, entertained.

I pull Scout close to me, and her barking ceases. Turning into a low, threatening growl.

"I don't think we've all had the chance to formally *meet.*" Max Blake smiles, menacingly.

He towers over me in height and weight. His dark blue eyes squint at me. He looks more like a UFC fighter than a senior in high school. He glares at me like I'm a bug he wants to squish. They're dressed in all black and between the three of them, I can't count the tattoos. I can see why people think they're a gang. They way they surrounded me, only leaving a few feet in between me and them, was intimidating.

"I'm Max," he starts.

"I *know* who you are," I interrupt.

"Feisty one," Joseph says.

He continues, unabashed. "That's me brother, Joseph," he gestures to his left. Joseph winks. "And this here, is Quinn," he says, gesturing to his right. Quinn shoots me a death glare.

"I'm charmed," I smile sarcastically. "Can I *go* now?"

"We never said you *couldn't*," Max chuckles.

I turn and start walking away.

"But since we're all *here*," he blurts out loudly, causing me to flinch. I stop, with my back turned towards them, pausing to listen. "I think we might as well discuss the elephant in the room."

I turn around, reluctantly. They walk up to me again, closing me in. Adrenaline starts pumping in my veins.

"We know you've got a thing for our baby brother, Benjamin," Joseph smiles.

"Maybe *he's* got a thing for *me*," I quip.

They all laugh hysterically.

"We just thought we'd warn you ahead of time. He's not really the "*commitment*" type, as you probably know," Quinn says.

I roll my eyes.

"We wouldn't want 'ya to get your little heart broken, now would we?" Max sneers.

"Not to mention, we don't think you'd be able to keep up with our kind of...*lifestyle*. Good girl that you are..." He leans forward and touches my hair. I flinch away and Scout snaps again, causing them to all jump back again. She barks viciously at them.

"It's not any of *your business* what happens between Ben and I." I grit my teeth down, irritated.

"Aw, she thinks they're a *couple*. How...*cute*." Quinn smirks.

"Actually, it's *all* my business." Max crosses his arms, his muscles bulging out of the sleeves of his shirt. I shudder at the sight of his huge fists and he smiles.

"Now, I'm *hoping* after our little *chat* today, that we can come to a little *understanding*...." he continues.

"That *being?*" I ask, hurriedly. I can't wait to get *far* away from them.

"Stay away from Ben," he commands.

My heart drops.

"You wouldn't want us to catch you out *alone* again. *Especially* without your little guard dog," he smiles, threateningly.

A frisson of fear runs through me.

"Let's go," he says to Joseph and Quinn.

They turn and walk away in the opposite direction.

I watch them until they're out of sight, then I run home with Scout. Ben just happens to be sitting outside on his front porch when I run past. He watches me with a look of confusion on his face, but I keep running. I unlock the door with trembling fingers and barge in. I slam it closed and lock it back immediately. Breathless, I head to the kitchen and pour myself a tall glass of water, gulping it down. Scout gulps her water from her bowl next to my feet. I move to the table and sit down. I drink my water, with my hands shaking.

I'm so angry and creeped at the same time.

How *dare* they!

Who do they think they *are?*

Threatening a teenage girl!

Trying to gang up on me like that?

Low-life jerks!

I hear a knock on the door and my heart leaps in my throat.

They're back?

I wait a moment and hear another knock. Scout growls. I walk slowly to the door to peek through the peep hole. But instead of the gang of brothers, I see Ben, standing alone and looking very nervous.

I open the door, only a crack, and peek out. "What do you want, Ben?" I ask, timidly.

His eyes drag up to mine slowly, they're wide and sincere. "Can I come in?" he asks, softly.

CHAPTER THIRTEEN

Visitor

As if it was even a question. They way he's staring up at me with his wide, deceptively innocent eyes, is already the answer.

"Um...*okay*," I say. I open the door more, stepping aside, allowing him to come in.

He looks around first, then ducks his head inside.

He just stands there awkwardly for a moment. Scout starts growling from her spot on the floor.

"Scout, no," I say, and she stops.

Ben watches her carefully, then turns to me.

"Your parents aren't home?" he guesses.

"You wouldn't be here if they were." I fight a smile.

"Oh, that's right," he smirks. "They don't *like* me...and neither does your *dog*, apparently."

"Yes," I wonder aloud. "Why do you think that is?"

"They know danger when they see it," he smiles.

I lose my breath for a moment, feeling nervous. For the first time, I'm starting to *believe* him.

His smile falls when he realizes something's wrong. "Something *happened?*" he guesses. "*What* happened?" he demands.

I look at the floor, fearing he can read my face.

"I *saw* you running," he reminds me.

"Can we talk in my room?" I ask, trying to avoid answering as long as I can.

That seems to cheer him up. "*Please*, lead the way," he smiles playfully.

I can't *believe* the way he's acting to me now, after he's treated me like a stranger to me for almost two weeks. But I still want to get him out of plain sight, in case for some reason my parents decide to come home unexpectedly. I turn and walk down the hall, feeling him follow me close behind. His presence in my house is making my stomach flip. Scout watches us with her eyes, suspiciously.

I open my door and abruptly become shy about letting him into my personal haven. It's very simple, just a TV, my bed and one dresser. My books are stacked in a neat pile under my bed. On my wall, hangs a cork screw pin-board, with pictures of me and Riley.

He walks in quietly, surveying the surroundings. I close the door silently behind him. It's so quiet. Scout scratches the door and whines behind it.

"Scout, *shh!*" I scold.

He walks up to the pin-board. "Who's that?" he points at Riley.

"My best friend back home, her name's Riley."

He nods. I feel so self-conscious, like this is some kind of test. I go to sit on my bed, realizing that there's no where else to sit in my bare room. Ben's icy eyes watch me.

"Do you...uh...want to sit down?" I ask him, sounding awkwardly formal.

He smirks. "Oh, why not?" he teases, but instead lies across my bed, lounging.

I'm surprised yet again by his abrupt playful mood change. He focuses all of his attention on me suddenly, making me feel vulnerable.

"*What?*" I ask, self-consciously.

He's about to answer, when the rose in my window sill catches his eye.

"Pretty flower," he comments.

"Yes it is." I watch his reaction, but he keeps his eyes downcast.

It's quiet a moment. He breaks the silence. "Are you going to answer me?"

I gaze down at my fingers. "About what?"

"You *know* what. Tell me what happened," he demands.

I'm taken aback by the sudden severity of his voice. I look up at him, alarmed, to find him staring at me. Noticing my reaction, his face softens. "*Please?*"

I sigh, deeply. "*Okay*, but I don't think you're going to *like* it," I warn him.

He waits patiently and I continue. "I was walking Scout and I ran into your brothers..."

He looks mortified. "Did they *hurt* you?" he sits up, alert. He picks up my arm, sending shockwaves through me. He checks it for any injuries, then he does the same thing to the other one.

"*No*," I mutter, bemused.

"Then what *happened?*" he questions me, his face concerned.

"They..." I still and look at him. His eyes are boring into mine with intensity. "They told me to stay away from you," I blurt out the words.

He closes his eyes and I can tell he's trying to rein in his anger. "Is that *all?*" he asks, in a measured voice.

"Well...pretty much," I shrug.

"What *else* did they say, *Abby?*" he pleads, suddenly taking my hands in his.

I sigh, he's not playing fair. "They said, 'I wouldn't want to be caught *unprotected* if I didn't listen'. "

He grits down his jaw, but continues to hold my hands, gently. He tries to hide the anger that flashes through his eyes.

"I'm sorry, Abby," he says softly, staring at my hands. "But if we were going to be friends, you would've had to find out anyway. My family isn't very...*welcoming*."

"*No crap*," I laugh. "So....we're *friends* again?" I raise a brow.

He sighs, his face grave. "Being my friend isn't exactly *easy*. As much as I'd like to say that my brothers were *joking*, they *weren't*. I *want* to be your friend, but I'll bring you nothing but trouble," he searches my eyes.

I laugh at how ridiculous he sounds. "You can't be *serious?* What's so *wrong* with us being *friends?*"

"What's *wrong* is, I don't want to be just your *friend*, Abby, and you don't want to be *mine*," his eyes blazed.

I lose my breath.

Of course I don't want to just be his friend, I just thought that was the only option.

I was confused about how he felt about me after all the awkward avoidance. But *now* it was pretty clear.

He scoots closer to me and my heart bumps, wildly. "I'm *dangerous* for you, Abby," he whispers, picking up a strand of my hair and twirling it through his fingers.

I'm confounded by his words. They don't match who he is *at all*. At least not the parts he's *shown* me. His eyes, so large and innocent, watch me. I'm reminded of his protective nature over me.

How could he *say* that? He can't *mean* it?

"*How?* You wouldn't *hurt* me, would you?" I breathe, afraid to know the answer.

"I wouldn't *try* to," he says softly.

I feel my eyes widen. My mouth falls open.

CHAPTER FOURTEEN
Dinner

Ben sighs. "I wouldn't hurt you *physically*, Abby. I'd *never* do *that*. I *want* to *protect* you. But at the same time, you just being around me puts you at risk. So in *that* way, I can't make any promises," he grimaces.

"*Oh*," I breathe, letting out the breath I was holding. "I get it now. Except, *why?* Can you *please* explain to me, *why* you're dangerous for me?" I hedge, carefully. It's what Ben keeps avoiding.

Why do we have to carry on like we're walking on eggshells?

He looks guarded at once. He leans back, away from me, withdrawing his hands. He's doing it again, avoiding telling me. I decide to try his technique. I slowly slide my hand back onto his, it seems to help. He closes his eyes and sighs, looking at our hands again.

"Ben," I say, encouraging to him to look at me. His eyes slide up to my face. I swallow to make the words come out. "Does it have to do with the curse?"

He pauses for a long moment, his eyes storming with deliberation. "Yes," he finally answers.

My heart pumps slowly in anticipation, as I gather the courage to ask him the scariest question. "Does the curse...effect...*you?*" I stammer for the right words.

"Yes," he whispers, his eyes growing wide with fear. Then he adds, "and those around me, *especially* those..." he trails off, hesitating.

"*Abby! We're home!*" I hear my mom call.

"*Crap!*" I say, panicking.

How did I not hear them pull up?

"It's no problem, love," Ben smiles, smoothly reaching beside him to unlock the window. He opens it easily and slips out, taking care not to knock over the vase containing the rose. "See you later," he winks.

Love?

He's never called me *that* before. I like the sound of it a little too much. I feel bereft. He's left me hanging,

I almost had *every* piece of information that I needed to know.

"Wait—" I call, just wanting to stall him from leaving a little bit longer. Despite the fact that he really *should* leave.

He waits.

"How did you know that I didn't have a screen?" I ask, stupidly.

He smirks at me, tilting his head to the side, as if to say *'come on.'*

My mom knocks on the door, sounding alarmed. "*Abigail*," she calls me by my full name.

He runs off playfully. I watch him as he slides his unlocked, also screenless window open, climbing in. Once inside, he waved at me. I covered up my mouth to contain my laugh. Then I slid my window shut, locked it and closed the curtains.

"*What, mom?*" I finally call. "*You can open the door*," I say.

She comes in cautiously, looking around. I'm propped up in my bed, holding a book, pretending to read.

She looks around. "I thought I heard you talking to someone." She scratches her head.

Panicked, I make up a lie quickly. "I *was*. I was FaceTime-ing with Riley."

She stares at me, trying to read my face. "Okay, honey," she says finally. She seems to be satisfied with what she assumes is innocence, in my expression. Then she changes the subject. "Remember that nice seafood me and dad went to last weekend?"

"Yes," I answer.

"Dad wants to take us all again *tonight*. So get ready!" she squeals, enthusiastically.

"*Oh*," I say, surprised. "Okay."

Her face drops. "Do you not want to *go?*" she asks, wounded.

"Of *course* I do, mom. I just thought I had homework for a minute. I forgot it's Friday," I smile, hoping she that she can't see right through me.

"*Yes*, it's Friday! So get ready!" she says, cheerfully.

She leaves the room, shutting my door behind her. I didn't really want to go out anywhere. I'd rather be alone right now, so I can process the flurry of thoughts running through my head. But I guess that'll have to wait. I sigh and put down my book. Then I get up and brush my now frizzy hair. I look down at what I'm wearing. I should probably change. My t-shirt and jeans most likely won't be appropriate for *this* restaurant. I emerge from my room a few minutes later, looking more polished. We all load into the truck and head to the city. My parents are right about the restaurant. It's right on the Williamette River, overlooking the water.

"*Wow*, what a *view*!" I say, impressed.

"I *told* you." My mom smiles proudly.

We get a seat by the window. The sun is out and is gleaming onto the water. My mom and dad sit down next to each other, leaving an empty seat next to me. The waiter comes and takes our order. I order the salmon. We're talking about my classes when I hear a familiar voice.

Is that...?

"Honey, *who* is that handsome young man *staring* at you?" My mom asks, suspiciously.

I look up, alarmed. Jamie is here, dressed sharply, not like I've seen him before.

What is *he* doing *here*?

He overhears my mom and walks over, his eyes on me.

"Mr. and Mrs. Brooks, I'm Jamie, Abby's friend," he smiles charismatically, extending his hand.

"Hi Abby," he grins at me. I half-wave back, awkwardly.

My mom's face lights up. My dad sits up straighter in his chair. Jamie shakes my mom's hand, delicately, then my dad's with a firmer grip.

"It's so nice to finally *meet* you, Jamie. I've been meaning to thank you for helping Abby when she was hurt," my mom gushes.

My dad looks more skeptical, watching their interaction in silence.

"It's no problem, Mrs. Brooks. Anything for Abby," he winks at me. "It's nice to meet both the both of you, too."

"So what are you doing here, *tonight?*" My mom pries. "Eating seafood, too? It's delicious here!"

"Hopefully," he smirks. "But first I have to work."

"Oh, you work *here?*" My mom asks, practically hanging onto his every word.

"Yes, this is my parents' place and I'm glad you like it," he smiles.

"Oh, your parents *own* it?" My mom beams.

"They do," he grins.

"How *lovely.*"

My mom is practically drooling. Me and my dad are basically just watching her converse with Jamie, because neither one of *us* could get a word in if we tried.

I clear my throat. "*Mom*, maybe you should let *Jamie* get back to *work*," I laugh, awkwardly.

"Oh. *I'm sorry*, Jamie. You probably need to get back to work, don't you? Here I was about to invite you to *eat* with us," she laughs.

He raises a brow. "*Actually*, I'm early and I'd *love* to," he turns to me and winks.

My mom looks delighted and my dad looks annoyed. I'm flushed and irritated. He pulls the chair out next to me. "*May I?*"

I try hard not to roll my eyes. "*By all means*," I smile.

The evening goes pretty well, minus the constant prodding from my mom to me, towards Jamie. He hooks us up with free appetizers, dessert and employee discount on the food, turning my dad into a fan of his also. By the end of the night, he has both of them practically eating out of the palm of his hand.

"Well, we'll go wait in the truck, honey. Give you two a chance to say *goodnight*," my mom says, trying to hide her goofy grin.

My dad watches us, not wanting to leave, but my mom pulls him by the hand. I hear him protest as she drags him away. Me and Jamie are facing each other in the entry way of the restaurant. It's glittered with white twinkle lights. Soft jazz music begins to play. I turn to see a band has set up for the night.

"We have live music on the weekends," he explains.

"Oh. This restaurant is *awesome*, your family must be proud of it."

He looks disappointed by my words. "Yeah, I guess."

"Thank you for tonight, Jamie, I really *do* appreciate it. My parents *love* you by the way," I smile.

"No problem, anytime. Guess it's a little harder to win *you* over..."

I feel a lump of guilt form in my throat. Jamie's such a nice guy and handsome, too. All he's done is nice things for me, even for my family. I feel ungrateful to not fully appreciate that. But the heart wants what the heart wants, and my heart wanted Benjamin. Even if he's not wealthy. Even if he's from the wrong side of the tracks. Even if he's all wrong for me. Even if he smokes, has tattoos and seems to break several laws. Even if his family is a house full of foul-mouthed, smoking, tattooed, law-breaking ruffians.

Even if he's cursed.

"Look, Jamie," I start.

"No need to *explain* anything to *me*," he holds his hands up, halting me. "Besides, I'm a *very* patient, *very* determined, guy," he smirks. I feel worry settle into my stomach. "I'm just glad you had a good time, and I got to be a part of it."

"Thanks again," I smile and hug him.

I run to my parents and wave to Jamie from the truck.

CHAPTER FIFTEEN

Bait

My mom won't stop raving about Jamie on the way home. Me and my dad both just continually agree with her about how great he is, both nodding and "*mm-hmm-ing*" at the appropriate times. We just want her to be quiet. When we get home, my parents go straight to bed, sufficiently satisfied for the night. I, however, can't sleep a wink. I toss and turn with Ben's words running through my head, until I give up and read a book. Eventually, I do fall asleep with my book in my hands. But I get woken up by the sound of Ben's loud brothers. From the sound of it, they're drinking and... *playing cards?* I look at the time on my phone

It's 2:15 a.m.!

I wonder where their aunt that Ben told me about, is? Working nights?

I realize that I've never actually *seen* her. Suddenly, I hear footsteps pounding down the hall.

Oh no, it's my *dad!*

He must've been woken up by the noise, too. I hear him grumble something as he passes by my door.

Great, so he's been woken up *and* he's angry.

I listen closely, acutely awake. I hear him slip on his slippers and open the front door.

Crap, crap, crap!

I don't want him going over there!

The thought of him challenging those ruffians frightens me. After the way they threatened me in the alley, it makes me wonder what other things they're capable of? I sit up in my bed at once, slipping on my Vans. I grab my parka and silently slip out of the front door. Scout tries to follow after me, whining behind the front door.

"*Shhh!*" I whisper to her.

Outside, it's dark and drizzling. I see my dad already standing at Ben's front door, bathed under the same ugly, yellow fluorescent lighting that we have on our front porch. He pounds hard on their front door. The loud laughing coming from inside, ceases and I see the door swing open. I hold my breath, watching. The eldest Blake, Max, answers, folding his giant arms over his chest.

"Where's your parents, son? I'd like to have a word with one of them." My dad demands.

"My parents are *dead*," Max says, bluntly.

My dad pauses, surprised by that answer. I can tell he wasn't expecting that. "Sorry to hear that, son," he falters for a moment. Max just shrugs. "Who *is* in charge of this house, then? Don't tell me it's *you*...?" My dad asks, in disbelief.

"Our aunt is, but she's asleep," Max answers.

"*How* could she *sleep* with all the *noise* you boys are making?" My dad asks, incredulous.

"She's a deep sleeper," Max smiles, undeterred.

Suddenly, Ben emerges from the doorway. "Sorry, about the noise, Mr. Brooks. We'll try to keep it down."

Max smiles down at his little brother, entertained.

My dad seems surprised by Ben's manners, or maybe it's the fact that Ben actually knew his last name that causes him to pause, briefly. But he recovers and speaks with authority again. "*Well*, I'd hope so. I wouldn't want to have to call the police...not that it'd be the *first* time they've been to your house." My dad lectures them both.

I put my face in my palm.

Ben nods, like he understands. I'm surprised that Max lets it slide. My dad turns and walks down the porch steps and makes his way back to our house. I hear Max say *"kiss ass"* as he punches Ben on the arm. I open the door and slide back in, undetected. I tip toe back to my room and close the door. I slip off my jacket and shoes and lie back down. I can't help but smile.

He cares about me!

The next morning, I wake up late, after having a rough night of sleep. My parents are going into town to go furniture shopping. They ask me if I want to go, but I tell them that I'm going to hang out with Meg today. I actually don't have any plans, but furniture shopping sounds absolutely boring. Besides, I was hoping to get another secret visit from Ben today. They leave and I hop into the bath. I soak and scrub for longer than necessary, butterflies floating in my stomach all the while. I keep thinking I'm going to hear a knock on the door. I get out of the tub and when I'm drying off, I hear my phone buzz. It's a message from Ben.

Busy today?

A huge smile spreads across my face. *Nope.* I text back.

Want to come over?

Sure. I text him. *But I have to get ready first.*

Okay. I'll leave my window open.

I laugh to myself. I have to go through the *window?*

I get dressed in leggings and a long t-shirt. I slip on my boots and blow dry my hair straight. I put on mascara and blush. I dig for a perfume and find a decent smelling one and spritz some on me. Then I go unlock my window, sliding it open. Scout looks at me strangely and whines.

"It's okay, girl. I'll be right back." I pat her head.

I slip out and slide it half closed through the outside. I walk to Ben's open window, I can see his back. He's holding something and moving his arms.

He's playing the *guitar?* I didn't know he played guitar.

I walk up to the window, feeling like I need to announce myself, but he already knows I'm there.

"Hi Abby," he says with his back turned toward me.

"Hi," I whisper from the window.

"You don't have to whisper, Abby. No one's home," he informs me. Then he turns around and grins a heart stopping grin at me.

"*Oh*," I breathe.

We're *alone* again? In *his* house?

"You can come in," he raises a brow at me. "I won't bite."

"*Ha ha*," I laugh, nervously and climb in. Ben puts his guitar aside and turns his attention to me.

Ben's room isn't messy, but it smells like cigarettes, liquor and his woodsy cologne. His walls are bare, besides an Irish flag he has proudly on display. There are stacks of drawings on his desk. He has a laptop and a much nicer TV than mine. I crinkle my nose at the stale liquor smell that lingers in the room. It must be from last night.

"Sorry about the smell," he smirks knowingly.

"Do *you* drink?" I raise my brow.

"My brothers do."

"But you smoke," I point out.

"A little," he shrugs and laughs.

I spot an old baseball bat in the corner of the room. "You play *baseball?*" I ask, curiously.

I find *that* hard to imagine.

"No," he replies.

I'm about to ask why he has the bat, when I realize that maybe I don't want to know. I sit down at his desk and look at the stack of drawings on it. I sift through them, slowly, noticing they're all very *dark*. One is of a woman crying, and the other is twisted up trees.

"Did you draw these?" I ask, still staring at them.

It's not until my fingers skim over the next one, that I let out a small gasp. He quickly puts his hands over mine, covering it a moment too late.

"Yeah, it's not a big deal, though. I just draw when I'm bored." He gathers the stack and takes it away from me, sliding it into a desk drawer. For once, *he* looks flustered.

But it's too late, he knows that I *saw* it. The last drawing I touched, it was of *me*. In the picture, I'm standing in the pouring rain, dripping wet, but smiling. The scene in the picture resembles the day I crashed my bike in the alley on my way home from school. The day Ben helped me. The day we first met. Ben runs his hands through his hair, is he actually *nervous*?

"So, where is everybody?" I ask.

"My brothers had some things to do, they won't be back until tonight," he answers, sitting on his bed.

"And your aunt?"

Ben looks surprised by my question, but he recovers and replies. "She's not here."

I nod my head.

Of course not. She must be a *horrible* guardian, she's never home.

I get up and sit down next to Ben.

"So, last night, sorry about my dad," I explain.

"That's okay. My brothers *were* being pretty loud. He reacted the way our neighbors *usually* do. All of our neighbors in the past have moved. Our family isn't very...'neighborly'," he shrugs.

"You don't say?" I joke and he chuckles.

"Well, I think you're stuck with me," I smile. "*We* won't be moving again."

"I'd be lucky to be stuck with you," Ben mutters.

His words take my breath away. He gazes at me, his blue eyes warm.

Time slows down again. He reaches up and touches my lips with his finger tips. Something strange comes over me and I lean forward, smashing my mouth onto his, kissing him desperately. He's initially surprised, but he doesn't stop me. He kisses me back, just as passionately. I run my hands through his hair for the first time, it's so soft to touch. He runs his hands through mine. Somehow we end up lying down on his bed, rolling around, messing up each other's hair. Our kisses become more urgent by the second. Suddenly, we hear a noise. We both stop and pull away, staring at each other, breathless.

We hear the front door open.

Ben's eyes widen in alarm. "It was a set up," he whispers, mostly to himself. "You have to go. *Now*," he commands.

CHAPTER SIXTEEN

The Curse

I get up at once, my heart beating wildly, and run to the window. But as soon as my fingers touch it, I jump back. Joseph and Quinn run up to the window suddenly, standing right outside of it.

"Aww, look at the love-birds," Quinn sneers.

I turn to look at Ben, not knowing what to do. I can hear Max's footsteps approaching.

Ben stands up and grabs my hand. "Come on," he urges, pulling me.

He opens the door to his room and we run out. We run through the house to the back door that leads to the backyard.

"We can go through the back gate," Ben huffs.

"Oh, *Benjamin...*?" I hear Max call from down the hall.

"I'm not going to *hurt* anyone. I just want to have a word with you and your little girlfriend....*together*," he taunts.

Ben swings open the back door, but before we can run out of it, Max catches Ben by the arm, yanking us both back. Our hands break apart and Ben pushes me out of the door.

"*Go!*" he yells, before him and Max struggle in the doorway.

I run outside, it's raining again. I spot the gate and run towards it. I'm almost there, when my foot catches something hard that I assume is a brick or a rock. I trip and fall, landing on my hands. I pick myself up, and am horrified to find what it *really* is. I read the words on the stone and I think I'm going to be sick.

Aunt Adeline, the grave stone reads.

I feel faint, like I'm going to pass out. My vision spins. Somehow I've ended up lying on the ground. I register, vaguely, that all of the brothers have caught up to me. Max is holding Ben by the arms. They stare down at me.

"Well, I guess you found our aunt," Max says, gravely.

"What are we going to do with her *now?*" I hear Joseph ask, but he sounds far away. "She knows too much."

I know I should be afraid, but I can't feel anything. Then everything goes black.

I wake up, confused.

Was that all a bad dream?

But then I realize, I'm still at Ben's. I'm in his living room. I'm sitting up in a chair, but something is off. I try to move my arms and realize that they're bound. My legs are, too. My eyes scan the room until

I find Ben sitting across it, looking much like me. I'm irate when I realize his mouth is duct taped. I'm about to yell, when I realize that mine is too. I wriggle in my chair furiously, nearly tipping it over. Ben's wide eyes watch me in alarm. He shakes his head 'no' at me.

"*Well, well,* look who's awake! The little trouble maker herself!" Max teases, emerging from the hallway. Joseph and Quinn follow behind, wearing bored expressions.

Do they not find this at all *alarming?* What kind of people *were* they?

Max is holding something in his hands.

My phone?

He punches in a text with his large fingers.

"*Yes, mom, I'm still with Meg. Can I spend the night at her house?*" he says, in a horrible impression of my voice. Then he hits send. He turns to me. "You are a *naughty* girl, *aren't* you? *Lying* to your mom about where you are," he smiles, shaking his head. "Well, it did make this easier for me," he shrugs.

I immediately regret not setting a lock code on my phone.

My phone buzzes with a new message and Max's eyes light up. "Ah, mom said *yes!*" he says, brightly.

My blood runs cold.

I'm not going *home* tonight?

What is he going to *do* with me?

Why is *Ben* tied up?

Was he going to hurt his own *brother?*

As if Max can read my mind, he answers my unspoken questions.

"Calm down, I don't plan to hurt either one of 'ya. I just tied you up so you wouldn't go screaming your head off to the police about what 'ya saw. And I tied up Ben there, because he would've never *allowed* it. He has been known to have a wee bit of a temper, as *all* of us Blake boys do. I didn't want him to go get his bat either, he's been known to swing it around. He's got a mean bat swing on him, that one and I don't relish the idea of fighting me own baby brother, either."

My eyes flit to Ben's for a moment, his look guarded.

So, that's what the bat is for?

But Max starts talking again and my gaze reluctantly returns to him.

"Now, I'm going to take off your tape so we can have a little talk now, okay? If you behave like a *good* little girl, I'll *leave* it off." He reaches over and rips it off. Ben twitches in his chair. My adrenaline is running so high, that I can't feel a thing.

"*You killed your aunt?*" I demand instantly. "*You murderers!*" I spat.

Beside me, I can hear Quinn laughing.

"*You're going to hell!*" I yell at all of them.

Max smirks. "Well that may be true, Sparky. But we didn't kill our aunt Adeline."

"What?" I ask, breathless. "But, she's *buried* in your *backyard!* I *saw* the grave!" I shout.

He continues, solemnly. "She died in her sleep last year. She was old and had a lot of health problems. She was a hell of a lush, too. She loved the drink." He pauses for a moment, smiling fondly, remembering.

"We didn't want to alert authorities because I didn't want child protective services splitting us up. It's *crucial* that we stay together," he says, emphatically. "So we had a little backyard burial for her. Just us, her family. That's how she would've wanted it anyway," he says, his voice thick with emotion for a moment.

The brothers look at each other. "Guess we have to *tell* her?" Joseph asks.

"Or we can make her go *missing?*" Quinn offers, all too cheerfully.

I pale. Ben shakes with rage in his chair, yelling something incoherent. His hair falls onto his sweaty forehead in spikes. I look over at him, stunned. He looks like a wild animal.

They all look at Max. He stares at me, I can feel him measuring my worth. I hope to myself that I make the cut.

He sighs, standing over me. "Alright, Sparky. Can you keep a secret?" I pause for a moment, then nod my head, feeling like a small child.

"Good," he says, speaking to me like I actually *am* a small child. "Because I'm going to tell you a little bedtime story," he smiles at me, but it doesn't touch his eyes. I look over at Ben, and he looks like he's in pain. He squeezes his eyes shut like he doesn't want to hear.

"A long time ago in Ireland, there lived a strapping young lad, named Cillian. His parents were weavers, and even though they weren't wealthy, they were happy. His best friend was his next door neighbor, a girl named Everly. Him and Everly did *everything* together, their parents assumed that one day they would be married. Secretly, it was something Everly wished for every day. It wasn't until they were teenagers, that something changed. Cillian started to show interest in other girls. *A lot* of other girls. He became somewhat of a philanderer. He didn't have time for Everly anymore, nor did he seem to care about her. She confronted Cillian about it one day, but he told her that he saw Everly more like a little sister. Everly's heart was broken and something *changed* inside of her. She caught Cillian alone one day, walking home from one of his lady's houses and asked to speak with him. She said if he didn't love her, then he would have to *kiss* her to prove it. Cillian did as she said, but when he pulled away, he fell to his feet, sick at once. He died that night in his sleep. The town was *outraged*. They looked everywhere for Everly, claiming she was a *witch*. But she was nowhere to be found. From then on, it was told that a *curse* was placed on the family. No son born under the Blake name would *ever* find love, and if he *did*, it would be taken away, tragically. He could have as many women as he wanted, lust and affairs. But once he came to *love* a woman, he could never *keep* her. For when he did, *terrible* things would come upon them. He would die lovesick or lonely. Everly's curse has rang true from then until today. So the question we want to know now is, does *Ben* love *you?*"

I look over at Ben, in horror. His eyes are apologetic. He hangs his head in shame. My heart races in my chest.

What will become of me if he *does?*

"Shall we ask him?" Max grows serious.

He's angry at his brother?
He's trying to *protect* me?
Trying to protect *us?*
He walks over to Ben and rips off the tape. "Well Benjamin, what do you have to *say?*"

CHAPTER SEVENTEEN
Punishment

Ben sighs. "I care for her, but I'm not in *love* with her," he says to Max only, not wanting to meet my eyes.

I breathe a sigh of relief, but inside I feel a little hurt. I know I shouldn't. It would be ridiculous for him to fall in love with me this early in our complicated...friendship/ relationship. But *still*...

"Good, there's still time then," Max sighs, heavily.

He sounds like he has the weight of the world on his shoulders. It must be hard for him to be in charge of his three younger brothers. But even more than that, to be the sole person responsible if they *live* or *die*.

"As for you, Sparky, is our secret safe with *you?*" he raises his eyebrows at me. I nod. "Good, then I can untie the both of you and you'll *behave?*" His eyes slide from my face to Ben's.

"Will you just bloody *untie* us already?" Ben breathes out, exasperated.

"Untie 'em, Joseph," Max orders, relenting.

Joseph fishes out his pocket knife and cuts the ropes binding our wrists and ankles.

"You have to stay here tonight. You can take the couch," Max points at it. "Ben," he calls, Ben stares daggers at him. "*You* stay in your room," Max commands him with a pointed look.

Ben nods, bitterly. He gets up and stares at me a moment, giving me a long look, before heading down the hallway, disappearing from my sight. I can't believe I have to stay *here* tonight. I'm *beyond* uncomfortable right now, I'm downright disturbed. Chilled to the *bone*. I'd feel safer sleeping in the *woods* right now. This house was the *last* place I *should* want to be right now. But for some idiotic reason, because *Ben* is here, I still want to be near him.

"We'll give you your girly little privacy now," Max grunts.

"Are we still ordering pizza?" Joseph asks.

Max laughs, harshly. "Well we can't forget the *pizza!*" he shouts, sarcastically. "After the *day* I've had, how could I forget something so important as *pizza?*" he barks at Joseph.

Joseph shrinks down, intimidated. Max rolls his eyes and sighs, "okay, we'll order the *damn* pizza!"

He looks at me. "What kind of pizza do you like, Sparky?"

We eat pizza in awkward silence at the table. I don't have any brothers, but from what I can tell, they're *disgusting*. They devour the pizza like Vikings, burping and gulping it down, loudly.

You would've thought it was some sort of a contest or a race. I try to avoid looking at them and *especially* try not to look at Ben. But since I can't avoid it *completely*, I peek up at him a few times, only to find him staring at me with an unreadable expression. I feel my cheeks burn hot each time it happens.

After we're done, Max tosses me a blanket and a pillow.

"Thanks," I mutter. He nods and retreats to his bedroom, following after his brothers.

I lie down on the stiff couch. It smells awful, like cigarettes, liquor and stale food. It's clear that I'm not going to get any sleep tonight. I can't help but pity all of them. The way they have been forced to live. The isolation, the paranoia, the loneliness. I still can't believe that Max has just been trying to *protect* me...from *Ben*. The way he acted in the alley, when he tried to scare me, it was all a bluff. This whole time, I thought Max and his brothers were the problem. I would've never guessed it would be *Ben, himself!* It's not like he hadn't been trying to warn me, though. The way he'd been acting made total sense now. *Now* I understand how he feels. He's my addiction and weakness at the same time. If I continue to be around him, it could be my undoing. My kiss of death. If he fell in love with me, his love would be like a poison to my body. A slow, sweet poison that would seep into my veins and flow through me until it stole my last breath. It would destroy me to be *with* him and destroy me to be *without* him. It just wasn't *fair*. But I would have to *try* now. I would have to *really* have to try to stay away from Ben. *My* life and *his* life depended on it. I would have to force all of the things I like about him out of my mind. His smile, his eyes, his laugh, his scent...I can forget them all. I *know* I can.

The next day, I awake to find all of the brothers gone, except for Max. He sits at the kitchen table, watching me. He's drinking a mug of coffee. "Coffee?" he offers.

"Please," I grumble.

He brings me a mug of steaming black coffee and shrugs. "Sorry, we don't have any creamer," he pauses, "or milk." I'm about to speak again when he adds. "Or sugar."

"That's okay." I sip my coffee. "Where did everyone *go?*" I ask.

"Work," he says.

"Ben *works?*" I wonder, aloud.

"We all do. Only on the weekends though, because of school," he explains. "We have to, since our aunt died. You know, to pay the bills."

"*Where?*" I ask, knowing I'm being too nosy.

"We work for a *private* company," he smiles a small, secret smile.

I want to ask more, but I get the feeling that I *shouldn't* or *wouldn't* want to know, so I just nod.

I finish the coffee and set the mug on the table. "I should go," I say, stretching to my feet.

Max nods, lighting a cigarette.

"Later, Sparky," he says.

I turn and walk towards the door.

"Abigail," he calls me by my real name now. I turn around.

"Remember what I said. This is *serious*, as *insane* as it all sounds. This is our *lives* at stake."

"I know," I nod, solemnly.

He pauses, shaking his head. "You're going to have to be the strong one. Ben is unnaturally drawn to you and it's going to be hard for him to fight. It's like you have some kind of *spell* on him."

I have a spell on *him?!?*

"What I mean is, you might have to be brutal. Do what you *have* to," he grimaces.

I gulp and nod.

I can do this, I can do this, I can do this, I chant to myself in my head.

I turn back around, walking out of their door for what sadly, might be the last time. But I whirl around when I hear voices approaching. I'm shocked to see Ben and his brothers walking towards me. Ben is carrying the bat I saw in his room yesterday. It has something on it.

Is that blood?

I remember Max's words about Ben being known "to swing a bat around", and shudder as I realize how *right* he is. Ben looks rougher than me, he's covered in sweat and has dark bags under his eyes. I guess I wasn't the only one who couldn't sleep last night. I glance behind him at his brothers, and they look much the same. My mouth dries, as I realize that the "private company" that Ben and his brothers work for, is on the *wrong* side of the law. Ben looks surprised to see me, he probably thought I'd already left. He walks past me without a word, though. A knot forms in my throat.

Who was I kidding?

This was going to be the hardest thing I'd ever *done.*

I walk over to my house and realize I need to put my game face on. I fix a false expression onto my face.

Look like a teenager who just came from a fun sleepover at her friend's, I tell myself.

I turn the doorknob and walk in, smiling.

"Hey honey! You're home!" My mom comes and hugs me. She crinkles her nose. "And you *smell! Abigail Brooks,* you smell like you spent the night in a *bar!* Have you been *drinking?*" She sniffs at me again. "And *smoking?*" she accuses, incredulous.

My dad's eyes snap up from his newspaper, assessing me harshly, from under his glasses. "The *hell* she *has!*" he shouts.

Crap, crap, crap. I smell like Ben's house! Damn my mom, and her over observant nose!

"No, mom, I..." But before I can answer, she's scolding me again.

"To your *room* young lady! You are *grounded. Indefinitely!*" She points down the hall.

I hang my head, realizing it's still better than if she knew the truth. I shudder at the thought of her ever knowing *those* dark secrets. I walk down the hall, listening to my mom and dad discussing what plan of action they should take for their delinquent daughter. I pass Scout.

"Hey girl," I reach out my hand to pet her. She backs away from me and growls. "Scout," I say. "It's *me.*" But she continues to back away from me and walks down the hall, all the while keeping her eyes on me. I sigh. "You *too?*" What is *her* problem?

I go into my room and lay down, exhausted. I pass out for a few hours. When I wake up, I take a long, hot bath. My stomach growls but I'm too afraid to leave my room for food. My phone buzzes and my heart stutters. But it's just Meg.

When were you going to tell me you spent the night at my house? ;)

I'm so busted. I text her back.

Sorry, I needed an alibi.

That's okay. We should really do that sometime, though.

I smile, glad she was being so cool about it.

Yeah, once I get ungrounded.

But I thought you were in the clear? She texts me.

Not when you come home smelling of booze and cigarettes. I text her back.

Ah, the Blake brothers, eh? So, dish. Does Ben wear boxers or briefs? lol

I cover my mouth to stifle my laugh. *I wouldn't know, we're friends.*

Sure you are! She texts me.

I sigh, wishing it was easy for me, like it was for Meg. She has a "normal" boyfriend.

I laid on my bed, with my hair wrapped up in a towel. Glancing out of my still half-opened window, I notice it's going to be another overcast day. My eye catches the rose that Ben gave me, still sitting in its vase. It hasn't wilted one bit.

How the hell is that thing still *alive?* I wonder to myself.

Kathey Gray

CHAPTER EIGHTEEN
Girls Night

I didn't mind being grounded. Although, it was worse when my mom took away my phone too. But intentionally avoiding Ben was the *real* punishment. Having to sit right next to him in class, and trying not to stare at him every day at lunch was difficult, but I still looked forward to it. We were back to "no contact" again. The most contact we'd had, was when he passed me a paper in Algebra II. Even then, he was careful to not touch my fingers with his.

"So I'm guessing you and pretty-boy Benjamin broke up, huh?" Meg finally asked on Wednesday.

I nodded.

"*Why?* I thought you were *crazy* about him?" She questioned me.

I shrugged. "My parents don't approve." At least that was true.

She choked. "Well, *why* not? What's not to *love?*" she giggled, sarcastically. It made me laugh, too.

* * *

The next day, my History teacher, Mrs. Allen, told us that we had a family tree project that would be due in two weeks. I didn't know much about my family history, but I thought it might be fun to do. At least it would be something to distract my mind from Ben. I rode my bike home with the sun on my shoulders. It was almost a warm day. I started my project at the kitchen table, filling in the blanks that I knew.

Abigail Brooks, daughter. Leonard Brooks, father. Natalie Johnson, mother. Father of Leonard, Frank Brooks. Mother of Leonard, Elizabeth Brooks.

I sighed and look down at my paper with all of its blank spaces. I didn't know anything else. I never knew my grandparents on my mom's side. My parents walk in the door as if on cue.

"Hey, sweetheart. Working on your homework?" My mom passes by me. She sets her purse on the table.

"Yeah. It's actually a school project. A family tree," I explain.

"Oh really, that's interesting," she smiles.

"Yeah. Do you think you can help me fill in some of these blanks?" I laugh.

"Sure! Let me see that pen," she grabs it from me and fills in what she knows.

Father of Natalie Johnson, Eric Johnson. Mother of Natalie Johnson, April Moreau. Father of Eric Johnson, Steve Johnson. Mother of Eric Johnson,

Nancy White. Father of April Moreau, Frederic Moreau. Mother of April Moreau, Emma Anley.

I look up at my mom. "Moreau, what's that?" I ask, curiously.

"French," my mom smiles, fondly. "My mother was French."

"What about Anley? Your grandmother's name was Emma Anley?" I ask.

"I don't know much about my grandmother, she died when I was little," she says, wistfully.

"Hmm. Well, I still have a lot of blanks to fill out but I have until next week to finish it."

My mom nods. "Good 'cause it may take a while to figure out."

* * *

I ride my bike to school the next day, feeling uninspired. Meg catches up with me, as I chain it up to the rack.

"When are you going to start accepting rides to school?" She stares down at me.

"I've actually started *enjoying* it," I smirk to myself.

"Well, you're in better shape than me, so more power to you," she jokes.

"*Hey*," she says, softly. I feel an annoyance creeping its way up my spine. She must be using that sympathetic voice for a reason. A reason I didn't want to know. Because if it's about Ben, I didn't want to talk about it. I look up at her.

"You want to go shopping with me this weekend? I just got my license and my mom gave me her old car. I've been *dying* to take it for a spin on my own. *No* boyfriends," she smirks.

"Good, because I don't *have* one," I laugh. "But...I don't know if my mom will *let* me. I'm supposed to be *grounded, remember?*" I remind her.

Her face falls. "Oh yeah, *duh.*"

"I'll still ask her though," I shrug.

"Cool," she smiles and grabs my hand, pulling me up. "Come on, let's go!" I giggle as she drags me along.

"What are you *doing?*" I laughed.

She pulls me along haphazardly, almost running me into several people, until I actually *do* bump into someone. Mine and Meg's hands broke apart and I turned around to apologize to whoever it was that I bumped into. But my breath catches when I realize it's Ben. He looks down quickly, trying to hide his face. But I'd already noticed that he has a black eye.

"Ben? What..." I start, confounded.

He turns and ducks out of the crowd, striding away from me, quickly. I sigh.

I guess I'm always going to have more questions than answers with him.

That night, I ask my mom if I can go with Meg. I'm sitting at the kitchen table, doing homework. Her back is turned towards me as she washes the dishes.

"Mom, I know you grounded me, but I was *wondering...*" I say, carefully. I recall the awkward conversation we had the night of my "grounding". I had to have the whole, painful "say no to drugs" speech, that I'd already had in grade school years ago. I had to explain to my parents that I didn't actually *do* any drugs and that I was telling the truth. They told me they believed me, but I know they still had their suspicions.

She half turned and cocked an eyebrow. "Yes?"

Suddenly, I have an idea. A *really* good one.

"Well, Meg just got her license and she wants to go out to eat with me at Jamie's parents' place and then maybe do a little shopping."

I'm smiling inside. I know how much my mom likes Jamie. If it was up to *her*, we'd probably be arranged to be *married*. It's like I said the *magic* name. I can see the side of her face, and her cheek lifts as she tries to hide her smile.

"Well, *I don't know*. Are you and Meghan planning to *drink* or *smoke* this time?" she tests me.

I have to bite my lip to keep myself from snapping. I find drinking and smoking to be absolutely disgusting. But arguing with her would not only make things worse, it would be an absolute waste of my time. Once my mother had it in her head that she was right, there was no changing her mind.

"*No* drinking or smoking. I promise." I shake my head from side to side. I already knew I had her when I mentioned Jamie's name.

She turned around and crossed her arms. "I *guess* that would okay," she sighs. "If your dad agrees." I knew I was in though, she'd find a way to convince my dad, for the sake of *Jamie.*

143

* * *

Benjamin was absent from school the next day. I was sad because I knew I wouldn't get to see much of him over the weekend. Every time I *did* catch a glimpse of him at his house, he'd turn away, hiding his handsome face from my all too eager eyes. When I thought about his black eye, it made my stomach turn with worry. I like to hope it was a silly accident that happened to him. But deep down, I knew better.

School seemed to drag. But when it finally let out, I rode my bike home excitedly. Meg was going to pick me up in thirty minutes. I couldn't wait until it was my turn to get *my* license. My parents kept putting it off, saying they would have to take a few days off in order to arrange it. I get home and park my bike. Walking inside, I notice my mom left my cell phone and some shopping money on the table. I smile at the sweet sentiment. I get ready quickly, changing into my skinny jeans, a cute t-shirt and my boots. I curl my hair, and put on a little makeup and perfume. I grab my purse and my jacket, then I hear honking outside. I stop to pet Scout, before locking up the house. Outside, Meg is beaming at me through the windshield of her small, used Honda Civic. I get in and she squeals.

"I'm *so* excited!"

"I can't tell," I smirk. "Just bring me back *alive*, okay?" I tease.

She slaps my arm, pretending to be offended. "Shut up!" she laughs.

Then she turns up the loud, chick music and we're off. The mall we go to is gigantic, with three stories full of stores that I've never been to or heard of. I start to wish my mom had given me more than forty dollars to shop with. I realize suddenly that I want a job. But I do manage to score a few affordable tops and a necklace. We decide to make good on my promise to my mom and go eat at Smith's Seafood, Jamie's parents' place. We load our bags into Meg's trunk, and I notice how many more bags *she* has than I do. As I'm walking around the car, I see someone who looks familiar. In the parking lot, off to the right, is some guy who bares an uncanny resemblance to Ben. I watch as the guy walks up to a very expensive, red sports car.

I think it's a Lamborghini?

I continue to stare, intrigued. He's dressed sharply, in a light tan-colored, tailored suit. He has on Ray Bans and equally expensive shoes. He presses the button on the keys and the lights of the car respond accordingly.

Meg suddenly notices too. "Abbs, what are you *staring* at?"

Just then, the Ben look-a-alike removes his shades, revealing a black eye. My mouth drops open and I gasp, aloud.

Meg's eyes follow mine. "*Holy crap!* Is that...is that *Ben?*"

CHAPTER NINETEEN
Savior

We watch in awe as Ben ducks his head inside the Lambo, climbing in. Then he shuts the door and drives off. He didn't even *notice* us. Meg directs her gaze onto me.

"What the hell was t*hat?*" she accuses.

For some strange reason, I feel guilty. Like *I'm* responsible for *his* actions. I shake it off, though.
"No idea."

I can't stop smiling like an idiot at the sight of Ben looking so sharp and suave. Deep down in my gut, I know that there is *no* good reason for him to be dressed like *tha*t, driving a *car* like that. But I try not to let it bother me too much. We both get in Meg's car and head to Smith's.

Jamie is working, of course. He's so excited to see us that he brings us crab cake appetizers on the house. When he walks away I confess to Meg. "I need a job," I frown. "I'm broke," I laugh.

"I need one, too," she agrees. "I like shopping too much," she laughs.

"Yes," I agree. "You *may* have a problem," I tease.

Her eyes grow wide with false surprise. "Shut up!" she smiles. "*Hey!*" she says, suddenly excited.

"What?"

"We should work *here!*" she says, her eyes alight with revelation.

I scrunch my face up. "*Why?*"

"*Jamie* can get us jobs! Waitresses *do* make great tips!" she says, enthusiastically. I'm about to object when she continues. "We can work the same shift and ride together every day!"

I couldn't really argue that point. That actually sounded pretty good. It would get me out of the house and help me to quit moping about Ben.

She bounces in her seat, grinning hugely. "So what do you think?"

"Sure," I smile, relenting. Just then, Jamie returns with our food. I turn to him. "Are you hiring?"

My mom is over the moon when she finds out that not only did I eat at Jamie's place, but I got a waitressing job there and I started on Monday.

"*I'm so proud of you!*" She had said.

Jamie's eyes were glowing when he gave me the job. It made me worry a little that maybe he thought it meant something else. But it did make me feel better that Meg would be there, too.

* * *

147

The next morning, I decided to take Scout for a walk. I was feeling pretty proud of myself for trying to behave like a responsible, normal teenager. I was just going to walk around my neighborhood this time. I was so occupied in my own thoughts, that I suddenly realized I didn't know where I was. A misty fog was starting to hover a few inches above the ground, it looked downright creepy. I fished my phone out of my pocket to call my mom, but my heart sank when I realized the battery was at 1%. I forgot to charge it last night. My mom picked up on the fourth ring.

"*Hello?*" I heard her say.

"*Mom—*" I said, but before I could finish, the call cut off.

I felt a panic slowly creeping its way up my spine, as my eyes searched for something vaguely familiar. When I came up with nothing, I started walking again, heading in no particular direction. I was just wandering aimlessly. The fog began to grow thicker. I felt like it was surrounding me, suffocating me. I could barely see the street ahead of me. I saw a shadow move and my heart stuttered. Scout starts growling low beside me. I'm frozen in place, while my eyes fight to focus. I stop breathing when my eyes catch sight of what's causing Scout to growl. A huge grey wolf is standing in front of us, it's snout low to the ground. It's eyes are predatory and the fur on it's back, is a pattern of matted and sticking up spiky fur. It begins to circle us slowly, deciding which angle would be best to attack us from. It wastes no time, lunging at us before I can form any kind of escape plan. I jump back, yanking Scout backward by her leash. A terrified shriek escapes my lips. But instead of attacking us, I hear a loud noise and the wolf simpers to the ground. I look around me, wondering. That's when I see another shadow approaching through the fog, this tine it's a *person*. My heartbeat picks back up.

"What the *bloody hell* are you doing out here in this fog? Trying to get yourself *killed?*" Ben scolds.

He's dressed in hunting clothes and is carrying a black gun with a long, skinny barrel. A cigarette hangs out of his lips, which are curved in an entertained smirk. I let out the breath I was holding.

Relief floods my body. Ben is here and he saved me... he also looks ridiculously hot.

"Thank you," I say, embarrassed. "Is it, is it *dead?*" I worry, suddenly. I don't *want* it to be dead, even though it *did* just try to kill me and my dog.

He lifts his leg and nudges it on its side. "Nah, it's just out." He shows me the dart in its side.

"So, that's a *tranquilizer* gun?" I ask, with my eyes wide.

"Yup," he says, crouching beside the wolf's beastly body. He pulls out the dart. "She'll be good as new in a few hours," he informs me.

"What were *you* doing out here?" I raise my eyebrows at his outfit.

"Besides saving your cute self?" He cocks an eyebrow at me. I flush. "I was hunting in the woods nearby," he says, pointing to the direction he came from. "I was on my way home."

"You were hunting with *that?*" I ask, confused.

"No, with *that*." He points to a rifle a few feet away, lying on the ground. "This one's only for emergencies," he winks.

"Well, I'm glad you had it," I breathe.

"You need to be more careful out here, you know. Just in case I'm not around to save you," he smiles, but it doesn't reach his eyes.

"I'm beginning to understand that." My eyes widen.

He goes to get his other gun, carrying one in each hand. "Let's get you home," he says.

Of course Ben knows the way back, easily. I actually strayed pretty far from my house. Scout even seems grateful to him, she hasn't growled at him the whole time. The walk back is awkward. Both of us have a lot to say, but neither one of us know how to, or *if* we should say it. I decide to break the silence.

"It's really nice to see you again," I say carefully, testing the waters.

He nods, his face grave. "You too." His jaw is strained. I can tell he's holding back so much. "But you need to stay away from me," he blurts out. "It's already *starting*..." he mumbles.

I turn to him. "*What* is?"

He stops walking and I follow suit. He gazes at me, his eyes serious.

"The curse is already working against us...haven't you *noticed?*"

"*No*, what do you mean?" I ask.

He runs his hand through his hair. "*Bad luck*, Abby. Have you had any *bad luck* lately?" he encourages me.

I think back. "Well, a little I guess," I admit.

"*What?* Explain *what* happened to you?" He waits.

"Well, I crashed my bike. I sprained my ankle and I almost got attacked by a wolf?" I offer, wondering where he's going with this.

He moves both of the guns to one hand and pinches the bridge of his nose. He sighs and closes his eyes. "And what do all those things have in *common*, Abby?"

I shrug. "I don't know."

He drops his hand and opens his eyes. "*Me*, Abby. They all happened when *I* was near. Whenever *I'm* near, *bad* things happen to you," he says, exasperated.

"What about *you?*" I point out.

"What?" he asks, distracted.

"Your black eye, how'd that happen?" I continue.

He shakes his head. "It doesn't matter, I brought that on myself."

"Have bad things been happening to you, *too?* Have you had bad luck?" I interrogate him further, beginning to worry.

"A little," he admits. "But that doesn't matter, protecting *you* is what's important."

"It matters to *me*," I argue, defiantly.

"Well it *shouldn't*, now drop it," he growls and starts walking ahead of me.

"What if I say it's too late?" I blurt out.

"*What?*" he stops and turns around to face me.

"It's too late," I breathe. "I *can't* leave you alone. You're all I think about," I confess.

"You don't *mean* that," he challenges, his eyes narrowed.

"*Yes,* I do. You can't just *stop* it, either! I'm already falling for you..." I say, shocking myself.

He looks momentarily shocked also, but recovers and makes his face hard again. "That's enough," he growls. "It's *never* too late," he says in a low voice, sounding mostly like he's trying to convince himself.

He won't talk to me for the rest of the walk home. When we get to our houses, he stalks off in the opposite direction to his house, refusing to walk me to the door or even tell me goodbye. I know I tested his limits, but I don't care. Everything I said was true and I know deep down, he wouldn't have been so angry, if he didn't feel the same way about me. Despite all of the danger in front of me, I can't help but feel hopeful about it. Things aren't over yet. Ben could be falling for me.

Our love would be toxic, but it would still be love.

CHAPTER TWENTY
History

The next week, I'm busier than usual. Getting in the routine of school and work is exhausting. Plus, I have my family tree project due soon and I still haven't gotten any further on it than the day I started it. Ben is ignoring me still, keeping steady on his promise to keep me "safe". Before I know it, it's the weekend. Me and Meg get off of work early on Friday night, and I ask her to drop me off somewhere different than my house, the Portland library.

"What are you going to do *here?*" she asks, curiously.

"Some research for my family tree," I explain.

I don't want to tell her that I don't have a computer at home. I would ask to borrow hers, but I'd rather be alone so I can concentrate.

"Well, how are you going to get home?" she asks, worriedly.

"I'll call my parents when I'm done. You don't need to worry about me," I smile.

"Okay, well call me when you get home," she insists.

"I will," I promise.

I get out of the car and wave to her as I walk away. Her car pulls off and I enter the building. I'm immediately overwhelmed by the scent of dusty, old books. I inhale it in, wondering if there's a single scent better in the world. The woman at the front desk notices me enter. She's of slight build with dark hair and a pleasant sounding, thick, foreign accent.

"Can I help you?" she smiles warmly.

"Yes, I need to do some research on the computer," I say, politely.

"Sign your name in here. You can have computer number four. When you're finished you can sign back out."

"Thank you," I respond and sign my name on the paper.

I go sit at the computer and type in Ancestry.com. I sign up for the free trial, fabricating the year I was born and type in what I know into the spaces provided. I'm more curious about my great grandmother's name, Emma Anley. I type it in and find out, in shock, that it's an Irish last name. Her mother was never married and her name was Ester Anley, my great, great grandmother. She gave her daughter her last name, I supposed. I dug further and find that she migrated from Ireland. I don't know why I start to feel a nervous feeling come over me. I find her parents after a while of clicking on the wrong things and reading information about different families.

Her mother was Italian and her father's name was Edward Anley. I click on the information regarding his family. His parents are William Anley of Belfast and Mary Agatha of Wales. I continue to follow the Anley name, curious to see how far the Irish goes in our family. William Anley's father name is Gregory Anley and his mother's name is...

Wait, that can't be right.

My heart drops low in my stomach and I feel like someone is sitting on my chest. I immediately start sweating, inexplicably. I look around me to see if anyone is watching, but everyone is going about their own business. I hit the print button on the computer and listen for a printer to come to life. I get up and follow the sound. I walk over to it and watch as it prints the fateful words. When it's done, I pull out the paper and stare at the words. I read them over and over again in my head, in utter disbelief. Almost as if I keep reading them enough, they might change. But they don't. There are the words, right in front of my face, in black and white.

Everly Jones

My five times great grandmother's name is Everly Jones. Everly isn't a very common name, so I have to only assume that she and the "Everly" from Max's story, are one in the same. There's not a doubt in my mind that *she* is the one responsible for the curse put on the Blake brothers, and their ancestors before them. The cause of all the sadness and misery they have suffered for years. She was a witch, they said.

Does that make *me* a witch?

A cold chill runs through my body from my head to my toes.

I have to tell Benjamin, I think to myself.

Maybe there's some way I can help break the curse? I sign my name back out and smack ten cents on the counter for the paper I printed, in a hurry to get out of there.

My mom comes to pick me up in the truck. I divulge all of the details, minus the one about Everly. She seems as surprised as I was that some of our ancestors are from Ireland. We don't have any redheads in our family, although we aren't the tannest people around either.

"I'm glad you finished your project." My mom smiles.

"Me too," I breathe.

When I get home, I head straight to my room to text Ben.

I need to talk you, ASAP.

He doesn't respond right away and I start to wonder if he's asleep. I check the time, it's 9:15 p.m. and already dark outside. I text Meg to let her know that I'm home, while I'm waiting for Ben to reply. I sigh, deeply and open up a book. It starts to rain quietly outside. I get through a few pages, before he finally responds.

I'm working. He texts me.

I scoff, insulted. I text him back. *Oh, you mean at your very important and possibly very illegal job?*

That's my business. He replies.

Fine. Can you just text me in the morning? I reply, tired of his moodiness.

Ok. Is all he has to offer.

I sigh and roll over onto my side. I can't *believe* I'm really related to Everly, it seems *impossible*. The thought chills me to the bone.

What are the odds that mine and Ben's path would *ever* cross? And that we would end up trying *not* to fall for each other?

Maybe Ben had it all *wrong*. Maybe the universe wasn't trying to pull us *apart*, maybe it was trying to bring us *together?* To *break* the curse...

I eventually fall asleep to the sound of the pitter-patter of the rain.

* * *

The next morning is Saturday. I wake, disoriented to Scout licking my face. She whines at my bedside.

"Ugh..." I grumble and roll over.

I scrunch my eyes shut, refusing to wake. Scout whines again. It isn't until I hear voices outside, that my eyes fly open. I lay listening to the commotion outside. I don't recognize any of the voices at first, but then I overhear my mom speaking with what sounds like an officer.

"*Does your daughter know Benjamin?*" An authoritative voice asks.

I sit up, alert at once.

"No," I hear my mom answer. "She's never mentioned him before."

"*Ma'am, we have reason to believe that she and Benjamin are friends. We have a witness that spotted them together last Sunday.*"

"*What?*" My mom asks, genuinely confused. "I think you've got the wrong girl," she insists.

"Either way ma'am, we would like to have a word with her."

"Okay," my mom says, reluctantly and calls for me, "*Abigail!*"

I get up slowly to my feet. Scout follows my lead. I have a very bad feeling. I knew something was amiss from the moment I awoke. Scout was trying to warn me. I push open my door and force my shaky legs forward. I make my way down the hallway towards the open front door. My parents are both standing there with a police officer. Red and blue lights flash in the background. I feel sick at once. I finally reach them and look up at them, afraid of what I'm about to hear.

"Yes?" I ask, nervously.

"Abigail," my mom says, gently. "Are you friends with the neighbor boy, Benjamin Blake?" she raises her eyebrows at me, questionably.

"*Why*, mom? What's *happened?*" I turn to her, trying to read the answer in her wide, concerned eyes. Fear is gripping my throat, threatening to choke me.

"Because he's *missing*, dear," she answers me.

I push past them in disbelief and take in the scene in horror. I hear the officer's voice behind me, calling me back, but he sounds far away. There are police cars in Ben's driveway, too. Max is on his front porch, talking to them. He glances my way for a moment, with an indecipherable look on his face. Down the street is a news crew, a woman is reporting with the cameras on her.

The officer's hand is on my shoulder now. "Abigail," he says, in an artificially soothing voice. I turn around reluctantly, trying to control my reaction.

"We know you're friends with Benjamin. We have his cell phone records. You were the last one to contact him."

I turn to look at my parents, who look completely flabbergasted.

"I'm going to need you to come with me." The officer says with a stern expression.

CHAPTER TWENTY-ONE

Interrogation

"Where are you taking her?" My mom demands, panicked.

"To the station for questioning. It's a standard procedure ma'am. We'll call you when we're finished."

"It's okay, mom," I assure her.

She nods, but the look of worry remains on her face. My dad just looks furious now that he knows that I deliberately disobeyed him.

* * *

The officer walks me over to the cruiser and opens the passenger door for me. I get in and look back at my parents who are still watching. I wave awkwardly at them, then turn around as we pull off. The ride to the station is quiet and tense. I assume that the officer is saving all of his questions for when we get there. He's a tall, thin man with short, dark hair and a thick mustache. We pull up to the station and get out of the car.

"This way," he commands.

I follow behind him, meekly, as he leads me inside of the building and into a small room.

"Sit there," he points to a chair.

I do as he says. He turns and walks to the door, but then stops and lingers with his hand on the doorknob. He turns back around.

"Do you, uh, want anything to drink? We have soda, coffee or water?" he asks, suddenly remembering his manners.

I shake my head. "No thanks." I feel too nauseous to want anything. He nods and leaves the room for a moment.

He returns and takes a seat across from me. "Alright, let's get started. I'm officer Callahan, by the way. This shouldn't take too long, as long as you're honest with me. We should be in and out of this thing in no time," he smiles, reassuringly.

I can't tell if he's being genuinely kind, but I nod and smile anyway. He picks up a clipboard with papers on it and snatches a pen. His eyes shift from friendly to cold in seconds, and his mouth sets into a stern line.

"Are you friends with Benjamin Blake?"

I don't know if I'm supposed to tell the truth or not. The way Max looked at me didn't exactly give anything *away*. But I *do* want to find Ben. I'm worried about what could've happened to him. I decide that it can't hurt too much to own up to being his friend only. Especially, since there was now "proof" of our friendship. A supposed witness and phone records. The officer waits.

I sigh, and finally answer. "Yes."

Officer Callahan allows himself a small smile, before getting back to business.

"For how long?"

"A few months," I shrug.

He makes a note on his paper.

"Are you aware of his criminal background?" He raises his eyebrows at me.

I can't help the puzzled reaction that must be written on my face. "No," I answer, honestly.

He looks pleased. "I thought not. Your parents told me that they warned you to stay away from him and his brothers. Why do you think they said that?" he prods.

I shrug. "Because they're *guys?*" I laugh.

The officer doesn't find it funny.

"No, it's because they're *trouble*. Benjamin and his brothers have been in and out of here numerous times for several different crimes. The only reason that they aren't all behind bars right now is because they're all juveniles. Well, except for the eldest one, I think he may be old enough for big boy jail now," he smirks, as if he's looking forward to his chance to put him in there.

I sit, waiting for him to get back to the actual questioning, impatient to leave.

"You're a *good* girl. I would hate to see you get into trouble because of those trouble-making boys," he warns, pointing at me with the pen in his hand.

"I understand," I agree, as if he has any actual say in the matter.

"Anyhow, when was the last time you saw Benjamin Blake?"

"Last Sunday," I answer.

The officer writes on the top paper he's holding. "What was he doing?"

"Hunting in the woods."

"Were you hunting also?"

"No."

He looks puzzled. "Then how did you see him?"

I smirk a little, recalling. "He saw *me*. I was walking my dog, Scout, around the neighborhood. A wolf had found us and was about to attack me and my dog."

The officer looks genuinely interested. "A wolf, you say?" I nod.

"So, I'm going to take it that Ben shot the wolf?" he grins, hoping he can charge Ben with something else.

"Yes, but only with a tranquilizer gun," I say, proud that it isn't the answer the officer wanted.

Officer Callahan frowns."Then what happened?"

"He walked me home."

"And you haven't seen him since then?"

"No."

"You weren't with him last night?"

"No, I was home."

"Can your parents attest to that?" he asks, writing something down.

"Yes."

"But you contacted him last night?" he mentions.

"I texted him, yes."

"About what?"

Now I *know* I have to lie about this. There's *no* way I could tell the officer the *actual* reason that I needed to speak to Ben so urgently, without looking like a crazy person. So I make something up.

"I wanted to see if he wanted to go to the movies with me."

"Well, that seems innocent enough," he smiles. "What did he say?"

"He said he was busy." I have to lie again.

"Doing what?"

"I don't know," I lie.

"Were you upset that he was too busy for you?"

Duh, of course.

But if I were to *admit* that, he'd use it against me. He's trying to trap me into looking suspicious, but I'm not falling for it.

"Not really," I answer honestly.

"Why not?" he watches me, carefully.

"Because it's *Ben*. That's his personality. I'm used to it," I say matter-of-factly.

"Then what did you talk about?"

"Nothing, I went to bed. He was supposed to text me in the morning."

He nods and writes down more information. I shift in my seat. He looks up at me again.

"Ms. Brooks, in your *opinion*, does Benjamin engage in any illegal activities?" he asks. He turns his eyes back down to his paper, waiting for my answer.

I think about him smoking, him driving off in the Lambo. "No," I lie.

He continues, undeterred. "In your opinion, do you think Benjamin engages in any *criminal* activities?" he looks back up at me.

I remember him carrying the bloody bat when he was coming home from a "job" with his brothers.

The image of him in that sharp suit that *no one* should be able to afford, walking up to the Lambo that I'm sure was *stolen* flashes through my mind. My throat dries up.

"No," I say, trying not to blink.

The officer sits back and sighs. "Well, I do appreciate your time and honesty up until this point. I just have one more question."

I wait, nervously.

Am I caught?

Is he going to throw *me* in jail for lying to protect Ben? He leans forward, watching my reaction, closely.

"Are you and Benjamin really just *friends?*" he eyes me suspiciously.

Even though I secretly wish to be his girlfriend, the unfortunate, all-too-true truth is...he won't have me. At least I don't have to lie about that, though.

"Yes."

CHAPTER TWENTY-TWO

Lost Boy

When I noticed that my dad had came alone to pick me up, I knew I was in trouble. This ride home would feel like the longest ride *ever*. I opened the truck door and climbed in, shutting it behind me. My dad didn't even *look* at me. He didn't even *speak* to me until after driving for a few minutes.

"I don't *ever* want to hear that you've been hanging around with that boy again," he says, in a chillingly cold voice.

I think for a moment before answering. "He's not that bad, dad. I know what people here say about him and his brothers, but if you knew their *real* story, I don't think..."

"*Enough*, Abigail. I don't care about their 'story'. They're *criminals*. They're *low-lifes*. They're *nothing* but *trouble*! You're too soft-hearted. You want to see the good in people, when sometimes no good *exists!*" he yells, losing his temper.

I bite my lip and my eyes water. Not because my feelings are hurt, but because of what he said about Ben and his family. He'll *never* understand. I can't argue with him more, though, without him getting angry enough to burst a blood vessel. I can't really blame him, though. He's just going by what he knows and sees. He'll never know their *true* story. I have to remind myself of that, to control my emotions.

He notices my tears and feels bad. "Awe, I'm sorry, baby girl. I didn't mean to lose my temper," he sighs, shaking his head. "I'm just trying to *protect* you. I can't keep you safe if you keep running around behind my back with that *dangerous* boy."

I nod. "I understand, dad. Maybe you're right."

"You're *damn* right, I am! I was young once, too. I know who's good company and who isn't. And that boy is *bad* company," he lectures.

"Okay, dad," I sigh.

"You stay *far* away from that boy and I'll make sure that he knows to stay far away from *you*," he warns.

"You mean if they find him?" I raise a speculative brow.

"I'm sure they will," he grunts. "I have a feeling those boys are like cockroaches, they can survive off of almost nothing and they're damn hard to get rid of."

I turn my head to hide my smirk, realizing that's the nicest thing I've heard my dad say about them.

We get home and my mom rushes over to me. "Are you *alright?* You didn't own up to anything you didn't do, *right?*" She stares into my eyes, her own filled with worry.

My dad, who's already had his fill of drama for the day, hangs up his coat, walks over to his recliner and kicks off his boots. He reaches for the remote and clicks the TV onto the football game. I can tell that he's going to be there for a while.

"I'm fine, mom and no I didn't. I'm just tired and hungry now," I say, sitting down at the kitchen table.

"Well here, I made lunch earlier. Let me get your sandwich out of the fridge." She hurries over to the refrigerator, opening it and taking out the plate. She walks swiftly back to me, setting it in front of me. I immediately unwrap the saran-wrapped chicken sandwich and dig in. Before I know it, she sets a glass of water down next to me, also.

"Thanks, mom," I say gratefully, between bites. I didn't even know how famished I truly was.

After I eat, I retire to my room to have some alone time with my thoughts. My phone buzzes and my heart stutters in my chest, but it slows back down, when I realize that it's only Meg.

Is your boyfriend really missing?

I sigh and text her back. *He's not my boyfriend...and yes they don't know where he is.*

That's crazy.

I know.

Maybe he'll miraculously show up at school tomorrow

Yeah, hopefully. I reply.

I set my phone back down and lie down on my bed. I pick up a book and try to read, but I find myself staring at the words without actually reading them. I turn on the TV and try to watch the one, corny soap opera that's on. Then I decide to take a bath to steady my nerves. I soak for longer than necessary, barely noticing when the water becomes lukewarm. I get out and get dressed in my warm pj's, robe and slippers. For some reason, I need the extra comfort today. I hear a familiar scratch on my door and walk over to it, letting Scout into my room. She puts her nose in my lap and stares up at me with sad eyes.

"It's okay, girl. I'm okay," I reassure her. But I can tell that even *she* can sense what I'm feeling. I beckon her to jump on my bed and she complies. We lie down together and I turn the TV back on. Now a movie is on, *Sleepless In Seattle.* I watch it, realizing it's actually a good movie. I don't remember drifting off, but I wake to the sound of soft knocking on my door. I open my eyes and find Scout's warm, furry body in my arms.

My mom peeks her head in. "We ordered pizza, hun," she informs me.

I reach over to move my curtain aside.

It's already night?

"Wow, I slept a while," I confess.

She smiles, sympathetically. "You had quite a day."

"Yeah, well I'm up now. C'mon girl, you want my pizza crust?" I say to Scout. She jumps up immediately.

We eat together and then I go back to bed. I lie in bed that night, hoping and praying that Ben will show up to school on Monday morning. But when

I'm almost asleep, a horrible thought crosses my mind. Ben disappeared right *after* I found out about my connection to the curse.

What if something bad happened to him, because of *me?* Maybe I wasn't *supposed* to find that out?

As weird as it sounds, I wondered if greater forces were working *against* me? After all, Ben had mentioned that "the curse" would work *against* us. My heart starts to feel cold, I have to stop myself before I think about it any further.

Stop being ridiculous, I think.

Everything is going to be fine, I try to reassure myself.

Ben is going to show up at school on Monday and everything will be fine.

Please show up at school, Ben. I beg him in my mind, as if he could hear me.

Please be okay. That Sunday passes painfully and uneventfully slow, with still no word from Ben. I can't wait for Monday to come.

* * *

Monday finally comes and I hurry to school, in search of Benjamin. My eyes scan the parking lot, front lawn, then the hallways. Then I see his brothers walking down the hall together, without him. I sulk my way to first period and stare at his empty seat. A woman's voice comes on the intercom.

"Students of Portland High, as you probably have heard, a student of ours has gone missing. If any of you has any information that can help, or need someone to talk to in this grave matter, our

guidance counselor will be available until five o'clock every day this week. We ask that you keep this student in your prayers and be respectful of the family in this time of need. Thank you and have a great day."

The whole class buzzes to life as I hear Benjamin's name whispered all over. I cover my ears to block it out. Thankfully my teacher, Mr. Tyler, calls the class to attention.

"Okay class, calm down. It's time to start today's assignment."

I'm grateful for the distraction of schoolwork. At lunch, I stare at Ben's empty table. After school, I have to work, unfortunately. But I'm so distracted, that I forget to bring someone's drink and appetizer, so I get stiffed on a tip. Meg drops me off and I start to walk inside, but stop when I see Joseph. He's sitting on his front porch, smoking. He looks deep in thought. I look around to see if my parents are watching. When I feel convinced that it's all clear, I whisper to him.

"*Joseph,*" I call.

He looks up and beckons me over. I shake my head, signaling that I can't. I don't want to get caught at their house. He nods like he understands.

"Max wants to talk to 'ya," he informs me.

I nod my head, feeling nervous inside. I hope I didn't do anything *wrong*.

I keep my voice down when I say, "I have to ride my bike to school every day. But I can walk tomorrow if he wants to join me?" I offer. He nods, in acceptance.

Suddenly, I see a motion in my front window. I abruptly turn my attention away from Joseph. The movement looked *a lot* like my mother's hand, brushing the curtain aside.

Perhaps she saw the exchange between me and Joseph? If she did, is going to rat me out to my dad? I wonder, in horror.

I guess there's only one way to find out. I walk up to my front door, turn the doorknob and walk inside.

CHAPTER TWENTY-THREE
Stitches

I walk in and neither one of my parents are there waiting for me. I wait and listen for one of their voices, but the house is quiet and seemingly empty. Confused, I call out.

"Mom? Dad?"

"*We're in here!*" I hear my mom call from my parents' bedroom.

Well, I'm definitely not going to go in there, I think. Guess I'm off the hook, then?

"Oh, okay. It was so quiet, I thought I was alone for a minute," I call. I pick at the collar of my shirt. "I'm going to change, I smell like *fish*," I complain.

I hear my mom giggle. I don't know what's going on in *there*, but as long as I'm not in trouble, I don't care.

The next morning, I get up extra early, anxious to meet up with Max. I want to know what he knows. Being in the dark and cut off from any information about Ben is killing me. I wait in the alley, until I see his burly figure round the corner.

"Okay Sparky, let's get this over with," he says, walking past me in long strides.

"*Wait up!*" I call. I'm still behind him when I complain in a huff. "What's your *hurry?*"

He turns around. "I'm a busy man, 'ya know. I'm searching for my missing kid brother and all," he explains. Then he resumes his fast stride.

My heart sinks at the emotion that causes Max's voice to uncharacteristically crack for a moment. He really is just a big teddy bear. A really scary, bald, tatted-up teddy bear. He loves his brother and his family, he'd do anything for them. I finally catch up to him and he slows his pace to match mine.

"You think you know where he is?" I ask, hopefully.

"We have an idea of where he *could* be," he pauses and gauges my optimistic expression. Then he continues, "but it doesn't look *good*," he informs me, his mouth in a thin line.

"What do you think happened to him?" I ask, holding my breath.

We both stop walking.

"Well, he said something to Joseph the day before he disappeared. Something along the lines of 'being tired of being bossed around', and that he was 'old enough to make his own decisions'. I think he wanted to prove a point. This was an act of rebellion, against *me*. A slap in the face." Max looks into my eyes with intensity. "He might've...went on a job without us. One we had all talked ourselves out of, because it was too dangerous for the *four* of us to attempt. We decided that the pay off just wasn't worth the risk. It was too dangerous."

My eyes grow wide. "How dangerous?"

He sighs. "Let me put it this way, I would've never involved the police if I wasn't worried that Ben might not come back *alive*. I was more willing to risk him going to jail for years, then for him to be with *these* people for another *minute*. If *that's* where he is, anyway."

I cover my mouth to contain my gasp. It takes me a full minute to recover, before I can ask another question. "So, what's the plan?"

Max laughs. "The plan for *you* is to keep quiet and let *us* do the dirty work. We're going to make our move soon, we just need some final details. We have some friends helping us with this. If things go good, I'll find a way to let you know."

"What happens if they go bad?" I can't help but ask.

He chuckles darkly. "Then we won't be coming *home*."

My mouth drops open.

"Aw, don't get all bent out of shape, Sparky. Don't you have *any* faith in us?" he teases. "By the way, I have a question for *you* now."

"What?"

He raises a brow at me. "What did you *tell* the police?"

After I tell Max word for word, what I told the police, he nods. "You did good. Keep quiet, though. If they come around asking you any more questions, you don't know *anything*. Got it?" I nod my head, vigorously.

We start walking again, and once we reach the school grounds, Max starts walking off in the opposite direction of me.

"*Max!*" I call.

He turns back around and raises his eyebrows, in expectation.

"*Good luck*," I say, a little quieter.

But he still hears me somehow.

He smiles broadly. "Are you *kidding* me?" he laughs. "I'm *Irish!*" he jokes, holding up his arms to the sky. Then he turns and walks off.

* * *

Two more excruciatingly, long days pass and Ben is still missing. I worry more and more every minute. I'm lying in bed, worrying about if he's alive or dead, my new disturbing nightly routine, when I hear a noise from outside. Car doors are opening and shutting. I listen through the dark, my senses hyper-alert, waiting to hear the sound of Ben's voice. I hear someone groan in pain and I sit up in my bed, staring into the darkness.

"*Hurry up! Get the Jack!*" Someone yells, but their voice is muffled by the walls.

A blood-curdling scream causes me to flinch in my bed.

Is it *Ben!?!?*

I open my curtains and see shadows moving behind Ben's curtains. The light is on in his room. I can see what looks like *all* of Ben's brothers' silhouettes, moving around Ben's room. They huddle around what I hope is Ben himself. I listen to see if the commotion next door has woke anyone in my household. Everyone seems to be sound asleep, though. I *know* I shouldn't go over there, but I just *can't* stay away.

Not if Ben is in there and suffering!

I slip on my shoes then I move my curtains aside and unlock my window. I slowly slide it open and climb out, carefully. Once outside, I get creeped out for a moment, worrying that maybe another wolf is lingering near. I will my eyes to focus in the darkness. When I feel brave enough to move, I tip toe through the blackness, towards the glow coming from Ben's window. I wait a moment, listening.

"*He needs to go to the hospital!*" Says one of Ben's brothers.

"*We can't take him there! It would be too suspicious!*" I recognize Max's voice, he sounds panicked.

"*He's bleeding too much!*" Another brother says.

Ben is in there! *Alive!*

For now, anyway.

I knock quietly on the window and hear the room grow silent. A moment later, I see Joseph's figure round the corner. He notices me and shakes his head. Then he gestures for me to follow him. I follow him inside of the house.

"Ben's *alive?*" I ask him, immediately.

He turns to face me. "Yes," he answers. "You didn't give us much time to get a hold of you," he shakes his head again, laughing a little.

"Sorry," I say quickly. "Can I see him?"

He pauses and lets out a breath. "I don't know if that's a good idea right now. We're kind of in the middle of something and...he doesn't look too great right now," he warns.

"What's happened to him?" I ask, afraid to hear the answer.

"Well, looks like he got shot one time and stabbed a few times. I'm not going to lie to you, it's a bloody mess in there. They busted up his face pretty bad too, I don't think you really want to see—"

"Shot *and* stabbed?" I gasp, cutting him off.

How can he say it say so *casually?*

He nods.

I gulp and he continues. "When we found him, it looked like he hadn't eaten since the day he'd gone missing. He was too weak to walk. We think..." he pauses, watching me carefully, wondering if he should tell me or not. I wait, unwavering. "They were torturing him," he finishes finally, his jaw strained. My mouth dries up and my stomach feels sick.

"I still want to see him," I stand my ground.

"Are you...*sure?*" he asks, skeptically.

"I'm sure," I nod.

He sighs, reluctantly. "Well, come on then." He leads the way to Ben's room. He opens the door, entering first and then announces. "Look who I found sneaking around outside."

I walk in and three pairs of blue eyes stare at me. But the only pair that *matters*, looks dazed and

178

confused. I tune out the voices around me as I take in the sight of Ben. It's heartbreaking. He looks skinny and sickly. His face is swollen and nearly unrecognizable. He's bleeding from his stomach and his leg. Blood is all over the bedsheets. I notice the bottle of Jack Daniels on the floor. They must've used it to sanitize his wounds. Max is kneeling beside Ben with a knife in his hand. The knife has blood on it. That's when I notice the area Max is hovering over. Ben's leg has fresh blood streaming through it. Beside Max's knees is a bowl containing a single bullet. I cringe when I realize what just happened, and realize that must've been when I heard Ben scream.

"What the hell is *she* doing here?" Quinn asks, infuriated.

"It doesn't matter," Max shakes his head. "She's on our side now."

Quinn glares at me from across the room.

"We need to figure out a way to close his wounds, he's losing too much blood," Max says frantically.

"I know how to *sew?*" I offer.

They all look up at me again.

"Do you have a sewing kit in the house?" I ask.

"Our Aunt Adeline did, in her room," Max remembers. "Joseph, go get it!" he orders, hurriedly.

"You got any more Jack?" I ask. "'Cause we're going to need it."

I walk slowly past the brothers, over to the bed where Ben is. He watches me through swollen lids. I sit down beside him carefully, scared to hurt any part of him somehow. He looks so *fragile.*

Joseph returns with the kit and another bottle of Jack. He also brought some kitchen towels. I take a deep breath.

"Got a lighter?"

In a house full of smokers, they all go to reach for their lighters at the same time. Three different lighters are shoved my way. I awkwardly pick the one in Joseph's hand. I use the flame to burn the tip of the needle, then I thread the string through. Ben is watching me intensely, I lean down and speak to him, softly.

"I'm going to stitch you up, okay, Ben?"

He nods slowly and closes his eyes.

Max grabs the other bottle of Jack, opens it and shoves it at Ben. "Drink up brother, you're going to *need* it."

Max holds it to his lips and leans Ben's head forward. Ben chugs a good lot of it down.

"Okay, let's get started," I say with determination.

I know this is going to be a long, painful night. But all I can think, is how grateful I am that he's alive.

CHAPTER TWENTY-FOUR

Sweet Nothings

"*Wake up*," someone nudges my side.

My body feels like it's made out of lead. I can't seem to open my eyes, so I ignore the voice.

"Amber, wake up before your parents come looking for you." The voice says.

My brain actually responds to that. I squint my sleepy eyes open and look around. I'm lying on top of Ben's bandaged up, shirtless chest. He's still sound asleep, in a Jack Daniels coma, no doubt. Embarrassed, I sit up and lean away from him at once. My cheeks burn hot, my face must look beet red. Someone laughs and I snap my head in their direction.

"No need to be shy around me, we're practically *family* now," Joseph laughs.

The other brothers aren't to be found. I ignore his comment.

"What time is it?" I ask, searching the room, frantically for my phone.

"Relax, it's only 4:30. You still have time to get out of here and in your own bed before your parents find out," he informs me.

I leap to my feet and scan the room again for my phone. Joseph smirks and hands it to me. I take it from him and go over to the window, sliding it open. I'm about to climb out of it, when Joseph's voice stops me.

"Hey, Amber."

I pause and turn around. "What?"

"Thanks...'ya know. For taking care of my brother last night," he stares at the floor.

"Anytime," I breathe, and hop out.

The sky is still deceptively dark as night. The grass is damp from the rain. I crouch down, looking through the windows of my house, searching for any signs that my parents are awake. The house still looks as dark and quiet as it was when I left. I creep over to my half-opened window and peek in. My door is still closed and everything looks the same. I climb in, and am immediately startled by the feel of my wet bedspread.

Duh, I left the window open and it rained.

I crawl over my wet bed, wetting the knees of my jeans in the process. Once inside, I close my window, careful not to make any noise. I lock it and slide the curtains back over. If I change the sheets, it might look too suspicious to my parents. So I walk over to my tiny closet and open it, getting out the quilt that my mom bought me last Christmas. I lay it on top of my wet bedspread. I slip off my shoes, shimmy off my jeans and change out of my smelly shirt that smells of booze and cigarettes. Courtesy of the Blake brothers, of course. I decide to spray my clothes with air freshener from my bathroom, in hopes that it'll mask the scent. My mom has already had her suspicions about me before, I don't want to give her *another* reason to question me. I put on an old t-shirt and pajama shorts and curl up in a ball on my bed. As I lie there, trying to ignore the feeling of dampness soaking through the quilt, I realize that was technically the *second* time I spent the night at Ben's house. Although, the *first* time wasn't exactly my fault. Since I was pretty much held against my will. I feel a twinge of guilt because I disobeyed my parents, but I have to justify my actions.

If I hadn't been there last night, who knows *what* could've happened to Ben?

The bloody, disturbing images flash in my mind. The way Ben looked when I first walked in. His blood-stained sheets. The way he winced, twitched and groaned in pain, while I did my best to sew up his wounds. Luckily, they weren't life threatening wounds after all. I shiver, recalling the stomach-turning experience. I *never* want to see him like that again. I surprised *myself* at how I was able to keep my cool. I *never* would've thought I was capable of doing something like *that*. Now he was sleeping it off, but it would take more than a night of rest for him to heal. It would probably be a few *weeks* before he looked normal enough to return to school again.

I wonder what the plan about *that* was?

Were they planning to *hide* the fact that Ben was home from the police?

What would happen *if* and *when* they were questioned?

What would they say?

The questions seemed to keep building in my head, but eventually, I fell into an exhausted sleep.

* * *

I wake up and feel odd at once. I'm uncomfortable and feel like something's off. I roll over and my whole back feels cold. Then I remember about my bed being wet. The rain-water soaked through the quilt, dampening my pajamas. I open my eyes and notice that my room is lit up by the sunlight. Too much sunlight. I grasp for my phone blindly, on the bed. My fingers finally find it and I pick it up.

It's dead!

I stumble out of bed and into the kitchen to check the clock. The clock reads 8:30.

I'm late to school!

I half-run, half-limp back to my room. Peeling off my damp pajamas, I throw on the first t-shirt I see. I pick up last night's jeans off of the floor and shove them on roughly. Thankfully, the knees of them have already dried. My hair is a damp, nappy, unfixable mess and I don't have time to brush it. I wind it into a messy bun on the top of my head. I slip on my Vans and grab my backpack, slinging it over my shoulder. I stuff my phone and charger into it on my way out the door. I walk outside to retrieve my bike and my jaw drops. Right next to my bike is a blue vintage De Rosa, with a red bow tied onto its handlebars. My Huffy bike looks so *plain* next to it. I walk over to inspect it and notice that there's a little brown tag hanging off of the handlebars, next to the bow. I lift it and read what's written underneath.

"*There is a charm about the forbidden that makes it unspeakably desirable*"

The words couldn't ring more true. I know that the note, along with the bike, is a gift from Ben. Although in his *condition*, I'm sure his brothers had to help retrieve it *and* deliver it.

In the early morning hours, no less!

I smile to myself as I imagine which one had to run the errand, it would be funny if it was Quinn, knowing his blatant distaste for me. I knew that Max and Joseph were at least thankful to me for what I did. The simple fact that Ben got me a present is flattering enough. But the quote that he wrote on the card makes me blush.

He finds me *desirable?*

Worried that my new bike will get stolen if I ride it to school, I hide it in the garage and take my old one. Even though I'm late and feel tired and disgusting from last night, I can't wipe the stupid smile off of my face as I ride to school.

CHAPTER TWENTY-FIVE
Trouble

I get wrote up for being late with no note. I worry that they'll call my parents, all I need is for them think to that I'm *more* trouble.

At lunch Meg asks. "What *happened* to you? You look *sick*," she cringes.
I decide that's the best excuse to explain how terrible I feel. "I feel awful," I nod in agreement.
She scoots further away from me. "I hope it's not contagious," she jokes.
I laugh. "I don't think it is."

After my work shift, I feel ten times more tired. I come home and start my homework for the weekend, but end up falling asleep halfway through. My mom shakes me awake, after what feels like only moments later.

"*Uggghhh, what mom?*" I complain. I squint my eyes open, barely being able to see. It still looks dark outside of my window. "What *time* is it?"

"They found Benjamin Blake," she whispers.

My heart seizes in my chest, even though I already knew he was home. I have to play it off like I don't already know, and like I really don't care either way. Even though, I think she's starting to get an idea that I *do*.

"Oh...good," I say, with little enthusiasm.

"They said he ran away, but decided to come back on his own. Then the most *awful* thing happened. He got jumped and robbed on his way back home," she continues, her eyes wide with concern.

Even though she's concerned, I can tell that she's pleased to be the one to be giving me the hot gossip.

"That *is* awful," I scrunch up my face, knowing the truth of what happened to him was *much* worse.

She nods her head. "He's starting school again next week. They said he looks awful, so try not to stare. Poor kid, it's not his fault that he has a terrible family."

I want to object once more, but I keep my lips sealed. "Okay, mom," I agree.

"Okay, well I have to go to work now," she sighs.

"Okay mom, love you," I say.

She kisses me on the forehead. "You too, hun."

* * *

Me and Meg work matching shifts on Saturday night, the restaurant is swamped for some reason. We hustle all night, making good money in tips. When I get home, I can hear my dad calling me.

"*Abigail*," he calls, tiredly.

"*Coming*," I answer.

I find him in the living room, sitting next to my mom on the couch. In front of them is my shiny, blue De Rosa bike from Ben, on full display. My mouth drops open and I swallow the dry lump in my throat, nervously.

"What's this?" He gestures to the bike.

My mom looks nervous.

How could I forget that I hid the bike in the garage?!

"It's, uh, a *gift?*" I attempt to explain.

"From *who?*" He narrows his eyes at me.

"From..." I pause, looking at my mom. She shakes her head, in the slightest motion. My dad doesn't notice, though. "Jamie," I lie.

"You mean, your *boss?*" He raises his eyebrows at me.

I'm about to argue that Jamie is my *friend*, not my boss, but then I realize that he's actually right. I nod my head, cautiously.

"That's hardly appropriate," he scolds.

I stand, staring, not knowing what to say. To my relief, my mom cuts in.

"Jamie's family *is* very wealthy," she points out. "He was probably just rewarding her... for being such an *excellent employee!*"

I want to slap myself. She tried, but she did not succeed. She's just as nervous as I am about this.

My dad turns to my mom. "Did you *read* the *note?* That's not something you write to a *friend* or an *employee!*" he fumes.

I take a deep breath and close my eyes.

Say what you have to, to keep Ben and his family safe, I think.

"I know dad, that's because we're dating also," I blurt out, not even recognizing my own voice.

Did he *buy that?* I sounded so fake, to myself. I see the look of shock register on his features.

"He's too *old* for you," he immediately accuses.

My mom is far too happy to interject. "He's only a junior."

My dad's head snaps back to hers. "You *knew* about this?" he raises his brows, his voice wounded.

"Well, I knew some about it," she pauses. "I didn't know about the *bike*, though," she smiles at me, mischievously. She turns back to my dad. "He's a very nice young man, give him a *chance*," she says in a soothing voice, reaching over to squeeze his shoulder.

It seems to calm him down, his shoulders drop a little.

Then he grumbles, "I still don't *like* it." I wait, wondering if I'm free to go. "Go put that thing back in the garage," he says, begrudgingly. I nod and do as I'm told.

I hope I didn't get Jamie in trouble now, I think. He's really just an innocent bystander in all this.

* * *

The next day is Sunday, so I have off of school and work. I'm excited to just stay at home and relax with Scout. I haven't seen or talked to Ben since Thursday and my patience has just about ran out. He's supposed to go back to school again tomorrow. Ever since he gave me the gift and love note, I've been wondering how things are going to be between us.

Have we finally reached the point that he's going to give in and we can be together?

Or are we going to go back to the whole cold and evasive thing we were doing before?

Furthermore, what's going to happen when I tell him *my* shocking news? I feel cold with worry at the thought.

I'm lying on my bed in my room, watching TV and petting Scout, when there's a knock on the front door. I stay laying down, assuming it's for my parents. Then I hear my mom open the door and greet someone.

"*Abigail*," she calls. "*Someone's here to see you.*"

What?

Who could *that* be?

Meg?

Ben wouldn't come to see me when he knew my parents were here, would he?

I jump up and rush into my bathroom, glancing at my reflection. My hair is frizzy and my mascara's smeared underneath my eyes.

Yeesh.

I smooth my hair and hastily wipe the mascara off with my fingers. I hurry to my door. I'm about to open it, when someone beats me to it. I gasp and step back and my eyes meet with...

"*Jamie*, what are *you* doing here?"

He smiles. "What do you mean? I came to visit my *girlfriend*." His green eyes are gleaming with entertainment.

My jaw drops.

"Oh, so you're as surprised as *I am* that we're *dating*? I thought it was just me," he chuckles.

My mom must've already mentioned something to Jamie about what I said yesterday, about us "dating". She was a little *too* excited about that fake news. I can't *believe* she *already* said something. This is *so* embarrassing.

"Come in."

I grab his hand, pulling him into my room. I quickly shut the door behind him.

"Things are moving so *fast*, I'm not that kind of guy," he jokes.

"*Shut up!*" I whisper loudly.

I turn to face him and sigh. "Why are you *really* here, Jamie?"

He leisurely walks over to my bed, sitting down and making himself at home.

"Well, I originally came over to drop off your check." He holds it out to me.

I walk over and reluctantly go to take it from him. But once my fingers touch it, he slides it out of my grasp, teasing me with it.

"But *now*...I feel inclined to stay," he winks at me playfully.

I narrow my eyes at him and he hands the check back to me, relenting.

"Nice room," he comments and I flush.

Jamie is obviously much wealthier than me and I know my room must look anything but *nice* to him.

"Look, Jamie..." I start.

"No, *you* look. Whatever *game* you're playing with your parents, whatever game you're playing with *me*, it can't be good," he says, irritated. I'm taken aback by his sudden change of mood. I'd never seen Jamie be anything but happy, goofy, and flirty. This was a side of him that I'd never seen before. "What are you *hiding*, Abby?" he narrows his eyes at me.

I turn away from his impenetrable stare. "It's none of your business," I breathe.

"First of all, you *made* it my business," he points out. "And secondly, I may be your "fake" boyfriend, but I'm your *real* friend."

I look up at him again, his green eyes are large and earnest.

"I *know* you are," I breathe. "And I appreciate that."

He pauses, looking down. "If you need someone to *talk* to, I'm right here, you know," he says, in a softer voice. I feel like I've been kicked in the gut. I know Jamie really does like me and he's being kinder to me than I deserve.

"That's sweet of you, Jamie. Thank you. But I'd just rather not talk about it...right *now*," I politely decline.

Jamie nods, knowingly. "Well, the offer's on the table all the same."

"Thank you, Jamie," I repeat, smiling at him.

He stands up. "I should go."

I nod and lead the way out of my room. I walk him out to the front door.

"Going so *soon?*" My mom asks as we pass her.

Jamie pauses. "Yeah, I have to go help my dad with something." He lies for me.

"Are you sure you don't want to stay for dinner?" My mom asks, sweetly.

My eyes bug out of my head at her. I'm glad my dad wasn't home to hear her say *that*.

"Thank you Mrs. Brooks, but I really have *do* have to go." Jamie smiles his signature charming smile at her.

"Okay, maybe next time. It was nice to see you again," she beams.

"You too, Mrs. Brooks," he says. Then he turns to follow me out the door.

His shiny car is sitting in my driveway. I turn to Jamie once we're outside.

"I didn't mean to include you in this, I'm sorry. I really appreciate you doing this for me, if there's ever anything that you need, that *I* can help you with—" I start, but Jamie cuts me off.

"Are you *kidding* me? That fact that I get to be your "pretend" boyfriend is good enough for me," he grins, playfully.

But the slight edge in his voice doesn't go unnoticed by me. Or the fact that his whole statement sounded purely sarcastic.

I laugh, uneasily. "Okay, Jamie."

He turns and starts to walk away, but suddenly whirls around. "I forgot something," he breathes.

"What did you forget?" I ask, ready to go back into my house to retrieve it for him. But instead, he takes three long strides to close the space between us and grabs my face in his hands.

"*This*." His eyes burn into mine.

He kisses me hard and passionately, dipping me and running his hands through my hair.

I pull back and gasp for air, staring at him, bewildered.

"*Now* we're square," he winks. "See you tomorrow." He puts his sunglasses on and walks back to his car, confidently.

I watch him get in and drive off.

Where the hell did that come from?

I can't help but feel a little...*violated*. Maybe "normal" boys were just as confusing as *cursed* ones, I think, ironically.

I gather my bearings and prepare to go back inside, when I spot something in my peripheral vision. Much to my mortification, I see Ben sitting on his front porch, smoking a cigarette. I'm relieved when I notice how much better he looks than the last time I saw him. He doesn't look as skinny and the swelling in his face is gone. He only has a few small visible cuts. He's healing fast. I want to go run over and hug him, but I stop myself. Our eyes meet and my stomach sinks, his blue eyes stare me down coldly.

He saw Jamie kiss me. He thinks we're *together?*

"*Ben!*" I call.

But he just gets up, flicks the butt of his cigarette into the air, and turns and walks back inside of his house.

Crap.

The Blake Brothers

CHAPTER TWENTY-SIX

Fight

I want to slap myself or cry with frustration after what happened with Jamie. I don't know why every time things start to make the slowest progress *ever* with Ben, something bad happens to throw me back to square one. It's like our relationship is on a game board spinner and I keep landing at "start at the beginning". Things couldn't have gone *worse* if it was planned.

Wait a minute.....was Ben sitting there the whole time and Jamie *knew* it?

Did Jamie kiss me just to rub it in Ben's face?

If so, I underestimated him.

Whatever the reason, it happened and now things are going to be *super* awkward when I see him at school.

I sigh and roll around in my bed. I'd been trying to get comfortable enough to sleep for hours, but I couldn't get the way that Ben looked at me out of my mind. I go to stretch and accidentally knock something over. I hear it clink onto the ground.

Scout barks from the living room. I grab my cell phone and put on the flashlight. I shine it to the corner of under my bed, to where the noise came from. I knocked over that old rose and vase that was in my window sill. I reach down to pick it up, careful not to prick my finger on one of its thorns this time. I prop it back up in the window, realizing it still hasn't wilted one bit. Carefully picking it out of the vase, I bring it to the light and inspect it closely. It appears freshly cut, *dewy* even. I touch the petals, and find that they're perfectly soft and smooth. I draw the rose up to my nose and inhale its fresh scent.

There is *no* way the rose should be so fresh still, Ben gave it to me *weeks* ago.

A chill runs through me.

It must have to do with the *curse!*

How *strange...*

I put the rose carefully back in its vase, thoroughly creeped out for the evening. But it does make me think... If that creepy rose can survive this long, maybe me and Ben can, too?

* * *

The next morning, I get up, ready face the day. Ready to face *Ben*. I go into the garage and get out the De Rosa bike. I rip off the tag and stuff it into my pocket. I can't help but admire it as I ride it to school. I chain up my new bike proudly and go to search for Ben. My eyes spot him and his crew of brothers getting out of their SUV. For some reason, he looks over at me. His eyes glance down at the bike and back at me again, then he looks away. People are already starting to stare and point at Ben. He ducks his head down, and his brothers huddle around him like his bodyguards as they walk. I follow after, in a vain attempt for him to talk to me. As I do, I can't help but overhear the whispering as he walks by.

"I heard he ran away because his brothers beat him."

"I heard they kicked him out because he didn't want to fight in their underground fight club anymore."

I scoff and roll my eyes. Ben must be *beyond* annoyed. He was only missing for a week, but all his disappearance did was generate *more* interest in his already intriguing existence.

First period goes like I guessed it would. Ben won't even *look* in my direction. Half of the class can't stop glancing at *him*. Despite their efforts, he remains stoic-faced throughout the whole class. I feel a little sorry for him, but can't help but admire his undying ability to block people out. But then, sadly, I also realize that's what he does to *me* all the time.

If coldness was a super power, Ben would be the ice *king*.

I watch him at lunch, eating by himself again. The bell rings and I decide to confront him. I follow him outside.

"*Ben!*" I call him.

He keeps walking.

"Ben, I *know* you hear me!"

I finally catch up to him and grab his shoulder. He shakes my hand off roughly. I put myself in front of him, so he has to face me. But when I see his face close up, some of my ferocity dies down. His beautiful face is still marred in a few spots and I almost make the mistake of crying.

"What do you *want?*" he spits out, angrily and I flinch back from the level of hatred in his voice.

It makes me shrink down slightly, my voice sounding small when it comes out. "I wanted to talk to you about what you saw," I plead.

"I *know* what I *saw*," his lips curl into a resentful grin. "No need to *explain* anything to me."

I'm about to argue, when I look up and see Jamie heading towards us.

Crap.

He waves at me and walks over, full swagger on display.

He puts his arm around me. "Hey babe," he says, not missing a beat.

He smiles down at me, then leans down to peck me on the lips. I turn as white as a ghost. Ben stiffens from where he stands.

Why is Jamie *doing* this? *He's taking it too far.*

"*Billy*, is it?" He directs his attention to Ben.

I'm almost too afraid to look at him, myself.

What is Jamie thinking?

Ben straightens up, and I can see the muscles in his neck tense. He smiles a slow, confident grin, leaning his head back as if he's about to laugh. "*Ben*, actually," he corrects Jamie.

"Oh, right. Well, *Ben*, I'm going to have to tell you to stay away from my girlfriend from now on, okay?" Jamie smiles, arrogantly.

He's talking down to Ben as if he were a child. It's the first time I've ever seen Jamie's 'entitled' side peeking through. I still can't believe he's taking this whole "fake dating" thing so far. I notice that we're drawing attention, as a crowd begins to gather around us.

They want to see a show.

I look around and spot Meg, standing a few feet behind Ben with her mouth hanging open. Max Blake is starting to make his way through the edges of the growing crowd.

*Oh no, oh no, oh no.....*I don't like where this is going.

Ben's eyes light up and he laughs. His reactions to Jamie's rude words and gestures is beginning to worry me. "Oh, *really*? And *why* is that?" he smiles, entertained.

I know what's going to happen if Jamie continues, so I try to warn him. "Jamie...*don't*," I mumble. But Jamie ignores me.

"Because she's too *good* to be seen hanging around *trash* like *you*," Jamie glares.

"Trash like me?" Ben's eyes narrow and his stance changes. I watch in terror, as his pale skin slowly turns redder. His muscular arms tense at his sides. His fingers twitch, then close into fists. "Abby, step aside," he commands. "Looks like I'm going to have to teach your *'boyfriend'* a lesson."

I do as he says, slipping out from underneath Jamie's arm immediately, too afraid to object. Jamie, too, looks ready to brawl. I make one last effort.

"*Ben...*" I beg him, in an effort to make him change his mind.

His eyes meet with mine for a moment, and I see tenderness there. My eyes beg him not to fight. But as he's distracted, Jamie punches him on the left side of the head. The blow makes an awful sound. The crowd, along with me, collectively gasps.

Ben winces and turns back to Jamie, he smiles a menacing smile. "You're going to have to *pay* for that, *pretty boy*," he growls. He turns back to me for moment. "You might want to look away now," he winks, and I know it's too late to stop it. But I can't avert my eyes away for some morbid reason.

Ben moves so fast that I can barely keep up. Although he's shorter than Jamie, he makes up for it in speed and muscle. He fights like a UFC fighter with no rules. I watch helplessly as he lands blow after blow onto Jamie. Jamie gets a few back at him, but not enough to match him. He seems mostly like he's just trying to block Ben's punches. People are cheering and yelling, but I feel sick. I can't believe I caused this disaster. Jamie gets Ben in the face again and Ben tackles him to the ground. Ben pins him down and pummels Jamie. Meg grabs my hand, startling me. She offers me a look of sympathy before both of our attention is back on the fight. Jamie stops fighting back for a second and I grow cold with fear.

"*Ben! Stop!*" I yell at him.

The raw panic is clear in my voice. Ben stops and looks up at my face, realizing his place. He looks almost unrecognizable, like a wild animal. His hair is a disheveled mess and he's covered in sweat and blood. Luckily for me, Max finally breaks through the crowd. He offers Ben his hand and Ben takes it, getting up from the ground. Max puts his arm around Ben's shoulders. Ben takes one last, long look at me, before letting Max lead him away from the crowd. Jamie looks like a bloody mess, lying crumpled on the ground. I can't help but feel sorry for him, even though technically, he asked for it. It's pretty embarrassing to be beat up by someone a grade under you. Just then, Mr. Tyler runs up, way too late. People start clearing out, like he's the police. He scans the crowd and his eyes land on Jamie.

"Who's responsible for *this?*" He points at Jamie.

The remaining people start to leave, too.

I realize with mild entertainment, *no one wants to snitch on the Blake brothers.*

Me and Meg start to walk away too, fading into the crowd. I take one last glance at Jamie. Mr. Tyler is beside him now, helping him up. When I see Jamie sitting up, I breathe a sigh of relief, he's *conscious.* More teachers start to appear. I search for Ben and Max, but I can't find them through the hectic sea of students and teachers. The teachers are yelling at us to get back to class.

As I make my way back, feeling slightly like a wildebeest in a herd, I hear someone mutter...

"Told you he was in a fight club."

CHAPTER TWENTY-SEVEN

Guilty

I didn't see Ben or Max for the remainder of the school day. Jamie was obviously absent from work also. But after what happened to him at school, who could *blame* him? I wonder if he was in the hospital or something? I wasn't sure of the extent of his injuries, after all.

I hope that his family wasn't thinking about suing Ben's family...

"Your life is like a soap opera," Meg had told me at work.

I sighed, in exhaustion. "That's more of an insult than a compliment."

She ignored my comment. "You're going to be the talk of school tomorrow, you know that right?" she smirked.

I stared at her, in horror. "I *hope* not," I breathed.

She raised her eyebrows at me. "You had the hottest *bad boy* in school, fighting the hottest *rich boy* in school, all over *you*. Now *everyone* will want to know about the *new* hot girl causing all the stir," she winked at me, teasing me. Then she took her tray and skipped off to the table she was serving, leaving me alone with those words.

After I got home, I texted Ben an apology. But I got no response, of course. I felt terrible for being the cause of all this chaos. Lately, I felt like I was the *sole* ingredient needed for *any* recipe to pure disaster.

* * *

The next day, I was nervous to see who showed up at school.

Maybe they would *both* be expelled?

I was relieved when I got to school and I didn't catch a sight of Jamie. I guess he needed more time to recuperate, or he was too embarrassed to show. Whatever the reason, I was dreading our reunion. I didn't think he was going to keep playing along with being my "fake boyfriend" anymore, either. Hopefully, I'd still have a *job* when he returned to work.

I spotted Ben in the hallway and tried to catch up to him in time, but the hallway is flooded with students. I lose him in the crowd.

At least he's not expelled?

I sigh, and make my way to class. But on my way, a short, red-headed girl stops me. She stares at me and asks, "aren't *you* Benjamin Blake's girlfriend?"

A shock runs through me as I realize Meg's words were ringing true.

"Ummm, *no*," I smile. "Sorry."

She eyes me, skeptically. "But I *saw* you yesterday, you were standing right in the middle of the fight. *You* were the girl they were fighting over," she says with more conviction. "*You're* the one who snagged *Benjamin Blake*." Her eyes shine with admiration.

"N-no, I didn't. I'm really *not*—" But before I can finish that sentence, another girl joins us. She's tall, skinny and blonde.

"*Oh my gosh*, you're *Abigail Brooks!* Where are you from again? Michigan?" she interrogates me, excitedly.

"Minnesota," I mumble.

"*Minnesota*, that's right. So *how* in the world did you meet *Benjamin?*" she asks me, with wide blue eyes.

"He's my neighbor," I answer, automatically. Quickly realizing, I probably shouldn't have answered at all.

"Your *neighbor?* That's so *naughty!*" she grins, widely.

"Yeah, but we're *not*—" I'm about to continue, when Meg steals me away, hooking her arm through mine.

"*Sorry* girls, we have to go to class," she smiles at them. They look offended.

"Thank you," I breathe, as she pulls me along.

"Hey, what are friends for?" she grins. "Besides, I saw the way they were cornering you, like two *vultures*," she scoffs.

I didn't want to have any more awkward conversations like *that*, again.

* * *

Today was the day I had to turn in my History project, my family tree. Which reminded me of the very necessary conversation that needed to happen between Ben and I.

But how could I tell him *now?*

He'd probably never speak to me again. Especially after everything that happened with Jamie. I get the feeling that I've lost all of his trust.

Our History teacher, Mrs. Allen, decided it would be a fun idea for a few of us to go to up to the front of the class to tell about our family trees. When she asked for volunteers, plenty of hands shot up. People who were proud of their heritages, and people who thought that *their* families were the most interesting. I also noticed plenty of people like *me*, cowering down in their seats, wanting nothing to do with it.

After a while into it, all of the 'volunteers' had went. Mrs. Allen started looking into the class for a few more participants. I swear teachers have some sort of sixth sense when it comes to this stuff, because of course, she called on me. After my face got hot, and I felt the strange prickly sensation run through my body, the usual feeling I got when being called on, I reluctantly went up to the front of the class. My hands were shaking as I began to name off my Irish ancestors. I peeked up for a moment, only to find the class was staring at me with more interest than I felt I deserved. Then I realize with chagrin, it's just because of what happened yesterday.

When I got to the top of my family tree, I wondered if I should say the name of the person that held so much weight in my conscious right now. I *longed* to say it, to set it free.

It's not like anyone would *know* anyway...

They wouldn't recognize or remember her name. Ben and his brothers weren't here, and no one would *tell* them, because no one knew the dark secrets that her name *held*. But when I, myself, said her name, I felt the weight of it.

"My five times great grandmother's name was Everly Jones, she was also born and raised in Ireland. That's as far as I got though..." I finished.

I left out the part about her being a *witch* though, of course.

My teacher started clapping politely and the rest of the class followed suit. Even though, *my* history may have seemed quite boring to others. Mrs. Allen suddenly looked past me.

"Can I help you, Mr. Blake?"

I felt a chill as cold as death run through me, as I felt the pressure of someone staring at my back. I swallowed nervously and slowly turned my body to face the *one* person that I dreaded to be standing there. But of course, with my luck, it was *Benjamin*.

How did I not hear him enter?

Had he *heard* what I said?

I realized quickly by his expression, that he had.

He looked shocked as he stood there in the doorway, note in hand. He didn't answer or move, so Mrs. Allen went and took the note from his hand. He stood there, staring at me, his eyes accusing and his mouth set in a flat line. He looked at me like I'd committed the ultimate betrayal. My expression must've looked so guilty.

"Thank you Mr. Blake. You may go now," Mrs. Allen added.

The class giggled, they probably thought it was a combination of us "dating" and what happened yesterday, that was causing this tension between us. Little did they know the true severity of this moment. I opened my mouth to speak, but realized there was nothing I could say to him in front of this audience of eager ears. I was powerless to defend myself. Ben glared at me with hate in his eyes and turned on his heel, shoving the door open that he stood at, and slamming it closed. I stared at the door, wanting to follow after him immediately.

"You may have a seat now, Abigail," Mrs. Allen says.

The class giggles again. I turn towards her. "May I use the restroom?"

She sighs. "Go get the bathroom pass."

I briskly walk to her desk to turn my paper in, then I grab the bathroom pass and try not to walk too quickly out of the door. Once the door closes, I spot Ben walking down the hall.

"*Ben!*" I call.

He pauses, turns around, glares at me, then turns back and keeps walking.

I watch him, as he practically stomps down the hall. I scan the halls for teachers or students. When I see that it's all clear, I start after him. I practically run after him, as I watch him shove open the doors that lead to outside, exiting the school. I reach the doors and check once more for witnesses. When I see no one, I drop the bathroom pass and push open the doors, following him. I don't care if I get caught anymore. I don't even care if my parents find out the truth about me and Ben. I'm tired of hiding and avoiding him.

I know what I want and I'm not afraid anymore.

CHAPTER TWENTY-EIGHT

The Storm

I walk outside and immediately notice the slate-grey colored clouds swirling dangerously overhead. The wind is blowing strong, and the trees bend under its pressure. My hair whips around my face as I search for Ben. I catch sight of him, entering the alley that I always take home. Thunder rolls loudly as I chase after him. As I enter the alleyway, I hear a loud crack above and lightning strikes through the sky, turning the clouds a deep purple for a moment. It starts to pour down rain, almost as if the lightning cracked open the clouds.

"*Ben!*" I call. "*Wait!*"

He keeps stalking down the alley, making no move to wait for me. I propel my legs forward and finally catch up to him. I run in front of him, forcing him to face me. He stops and I notice his hands are shaking with rage.

"Get away from me Abigail, I don't want to hurt you," he growls.

I feel a hit to my heart, but continue anyway. "*Please listen* to me, Ben!" I plead, on the verge of tears.

The rain is pouring down so hard that we're both already drenched.

"About *what?*" he narrows his eyes at me dangerously. "I know *everything* I need to know. It all makes *sense* now," he shakes his head, smiling sardonically. "The reason I couldn't leave you alone. You had me under some sort of *sick* love spell. The apple doesn't fall far from the tree, *does it?*" he accuses with disgust.

"What are you *saying?*" I ask, in disbelief. "You think I'm *like her?* You think *I'm*..." I trail off, not being able to say the word.

"A *witch?*" Ben finishes for me, tilting his head to one side. His blue eyes pierce through me, like knives. "I *know* you are...why else would I fall for you so *fast?*" he admits, accidentally revealing too much. His harsh façade slips for a moment and he looks embarrassed. When he recovers, his face is hard again. "You're *just* like *her.*"

"I'm *not* a *witch!*" I yell at him with tears burning in my eyes.

"I can't *believe* you didn't *tell* me," he looks at the ground, shaking his head. Then he looks up and his expression changes to one of pain. "Then again, why *would* you? You had me *right* where you wanted me. I *trusted* you!" he yells suddenly, causing me to flinch. His face is full of betrayal, regret shines in his eyes and his mouth is set into a thin, flat line.

"I *tried* to tell you!" I argue. "You wouldn't *talk* to me, *remember?* You wouldn't let me in through your *stone walls*, long enough to!" I fume, all of the pent up frustration that I'd held back, suddenly exploding at once. "Then you went *missing*, so I *couldn't!* And then you stopped talking to me *again!*" I yell, exasperated. I feel like the breath is being sucked from my lungs. He stares at me, realization dawning in his eyes. I calm down and take a deep breath. "I would *never* try to *'trick'* you into feeling something for me, either," I say, much more softly.

He pauses. "How long did you *know?*" he furrows his brows. I can tell that his anger is slowly dissipating. His moment of irrational rage, fading.

"I found out about a week ago, right before you disappeared," I inform him.

"So you didn't know about it *until* then?" he asks, sounding the tiniest bit, less disappointed.

I shake my head. "I was more shocked than you," I confess. "But it *did* make me wonder...if it was *my* family that started this whole mess, maybe *my* family, or *I* can end it?" I say, breathlessly. "I mean, there *has* to be a reason why we met and were so drawn to each other? Maybe we were *meant* to? Maybe we can break the curse?" I theorize, further.

He grows quiet in thought. His features flashing in a range of emotions. I take his moment of deliberation to ask what has been bothering me for a while. Since we were putting *everything* on the table, I figured it was *his* turn to come clean. "*Ben...where* did you go? When you were missing, your brothers won't tell me. Will you tell me what *happened* to you?"

"This isn't the time," he shakes his head at me.

I throw my hands in the air. "It's never the right *time* with you! *I'm* the one who stitched up your injuries, don't you think I should have the *right* to know how you got them?" I beg. His jaw tenses, but he says nothing, keeping his expression unreadable. I start to pace in frustration. "I *saw* you wearing that *freaking* suit, you know? Getting into that *Lamborghini!* Who *does* that? You're only *sixteen!* Are you secretly *rich* or a *damn* good criminal?" My head snaps to him and he pales. I continue on my rant, all of my words spilling out now, uncontrollably. "I saw you carrying home a *bloody* baseball bat! Did you *kill* someone? Is that what you do on your *'jobs'?*" When I turn to face him again, his mouth is hanging open in shock. I stop pacing and stand in front of him, taking a deep breath. "I'm tired of all the *secrets*, Ben. You know all of *mine*. When are *you* going to confess *yours?*" I plead with him. I felt good to get it all off of my chest.

He looks taken aback by my sudden outburst, but quickly schools his features. "I guess I *do* owe you a few explanations... and we'll get to that," he swallows. "I didn't know you saw me in the Lamborghini either," he looks nervous. He runs his hands through his wet hair, distracting me. Then he furrows his brows. "Can we talk about it *later?*" he pleads, desperately. "You know, when it's not *pouring* buckets on us? It may take a *while* to explain." I think about it for a minute, I guess it's not a completely irrational point.

I nod. "Only if *promise* you're going to explain *everything*."

His face is grave. "I *promise*...but you need to *know*, by me telling you, I'm putting *your* safety at risk. That's why I've never told you before."

"*Oh*..." My face falls.

"Yeah, *'oh'*, believe it or not, I actually *do* care about what happens to you," he smirks, but the smile doesn't touch his eyes. He looks sad.

"I care about you, *too*," I breathe.

Somehow, all of our anger has melted away. The storm, too, seems to dull down. The rain is down to a light sprinkle.

"Do you *really* think you can break the curse?" he asks, hopeful.

"I'm *sure* there's a way. I mean, I'm not a *witch* or anything. But if love *started* the spell, then surely love can *end* it? We have to have faith in *something*, right?" I try to smile. But inside, I'm terrified.

What if I *can't* break it and Ben will realize it and want *nothing* to do with me? I was running off of faith and desperation.

"*How?*" He watches me, unsure. "H*ow* can we break it?" he seems determined.

I think for a minute. "Well, what have we been doing so far? Avoiding each other, not talking, not touching or..." I pause, my cheeks burning. "....Kissing," I finish. I suddenly feel too much pressure and want to turn away. "What I *mean* is," I clear my throat, my cheeks burning. 'We've been *fighting* our feelings for each other," I blurt out.

I peek up at him and he looks affected, his eyes are wide. He gulps. "You're right," he says.

Suddenly, I need to know for sure. "Do you..." I stutter. "Do you still... feel the same...about *me?*" I stare down at my hands, nervous to hear the answer.

"*Definitely,*" he breathes. "I wouldn't fight a bloke unless I was *crazy* about someone."

I look up. "You're...*crazy* about me?" My lips twitch.

"*Absolutely deranged,*" he smiles widely, his blue eyes shining. "Crazy enough to think that you had me under *a spell,*" he laughs. I can't help the responding grin that I feel breaking onto my face. "*And...*" he asks. "I'm assuming you still fancy *me?*" he smirks, raising a brow, inquiring.

"Do you *really* need to ask that?" I counter. "I think it's kind of *obvious,*" my face flames. He laughs and then pauses, looking nervous again. "Okay...so now that we're clear on *that*. What were you saying we should...*um...do?*" he clears his throat.

I get all flustered again. "I...I think we should do the *opposite* of what we've *been...* um, doing," I struggle. "We've been holding *everything* back...I think we should..."

"*Let go?*" he answers for me, his voice husky.

I look up to see his eyes wide. "*Yes,*" I answer. He gulps. I slowly step closer to him, our faces only inches away. "Do you *trust* me?" I ask, in a rare moment of pure confidence.

He clears his throat before answering. "*Yes.*"

Before I even know what I'm doing, my whole body draws to Ben with a craving I'm unfamiliar with. I press my body against his and wrap my arms around his neck as our lips meet. He tentatively reaches his arms around my waist, before embracing me tightly. We both finally let go of everything we were holding in, our lips becoming urgent against each other's. I get the floaty feeling like I'm dreaming again as we kiss. I've been waiting *so* long for just *one* more kiss from him, it only makes the moment that much sweeter. We break away from each other, gasping for air, gazing into each other's eyes, in wonder.

That's when I feel it.

The hair on my arms and the back of my neck stands up. Ben's damp hair is also standing on end as he smiles at me. I feel the unmistakable feeling of electricity in the air. Not just from our passionate kiss, but from *actual* electricity. It seems like time slows down. I look up in terror, as the white-hot light cracks through the sky above our heads. Ben, lost in the moment, doesn't see it coming. I shove Ben back with all the force I can muster, before the lightning bolt shoots downward and jolts into my body. I hear Ben scream in the background, as Mother Nature claims me.

"*Abby! No!*" he sounds tortured.

Sorry, Ben.

My body feels like it's paralyzed in a fire. The heat is overwhelming. My limbs ache so badly, that I think my body is going to implode from the pain. I feel like the electricity itself, has suspended my body in the air. Even though the pain should be mind numbing, somehow I can still process thoughts.

I guess this is how I die.

He warned me and still, I persisted.

I had to pick the *one* guy that I couldn't have.

I believed in vain that I could *save* him.

I believed I could save myself.

All in the name of *love.*

What a *fool* I was, thinking that *I* could break a century-old curse.

Who was *I* anyway? Just a normal girl, no one special.

Now my parents would have to bury their only daughter. I was sorry for that.

They would never know the *truth.*

Maybe they could have *another* child? Try again? For a better child, who doesn't want *ridiculous* things. Someone who has *regular* life goals.

Someone new to play with Scout.

I let Ben down, too. I convinced him that I was strong enough. At least I saved *his* life, that had to count for something. His brothers would be proud.

Was it *worth it,* though?

Would I do it all *again,* if given the choice?

In a heartbeat.

But I guess, *you win, Everly.*

That's the last thought I have, before everything goes black.

CHAPTER TWENTY-NINE
New Day

"It's amazing that she's even *alive*. For a girl as young as her and of her *size*, she must be built pretty tough." I hear a voice say.

"Like her *dad*." I recognize my mother's voice.

Am I in *heaven?*

If I am, then why is everything *dark*?

Why can't I *move?*

I try to move my hand, feeling it twitch slightly.

"Did you see *that?*" My mom says.

"See *what?*" My dad asks.

"Her *hand!* It *moved!*" My mom's voice is full of hope.

Wait, I'm *alive?*

I try to move my feet, I wiggle my right foot.

"She's waking up!" My mom gasps. "Benjamin, come *here!*"

Benjamin?

If my mom is *knowingly* befriending Benjamin, then I *must* be dead. There is no way that my dad would even let him *near* me.

"*Abby*...can you...can you hear me?" Ben asks.
Ben is here!
I try to say his name.
"*Mmmm*..." Is all that comes out.
"Oh my gosh! Abby, *honey*, wake up! Me and your dad have been *so* worried!" My mom begs.
Suddenly, I hear a foreign voice. "Abigail, I'm Dr. Thomason, if you can hear me, move your hand."
I wiggle my fingers, slowly. I fight to open my eyes, my body feels so *weak*. But my eyes finally squint open, and I scan my surroundings. I'm in the hospital, wearing a gown and lying on a white bed. My mom is sitting on one side of the bed, with my dad standing behind her. The doctor is standing on the other side of the bed, and Ben is standing behind him.
Everyone looks so *worried.*
The doctor is a man who looks to be in his thirties, with dark hair and eyes. He steps forward to check my vitals. He shines a light in my eyes and has me do a few simple tests, before recording everything on his clipboard.
"You're a *very* lucky girl," he smiles. "Not many can say they got struck by lightning and *live* to tell about it."
I nod, slowly, in agreement.
I guess that means I passed his tests?
He leaves the room to give us privacy.
I turn to my mom and dad. "Mom, dad, I'm so *sorry.*" Tears brim in my eyes.
"It's okay, honey. It isn't your fault. We're just happy that you're *okay.*" My mom cups my face in her hands.

My dad steps forward and gently holds my hand. "Struck by lightning and *still* kicking. That's my girl," he beams, proudly. I smile at him. "Glad you're okay, baby girl," he smiles, emotion leaking into his voice.

"Thanks, dad," I say.

I turn to Ben, who's watching me warily. Both of his hands are stuffed into his front jean pockets.

"*Benjamin*," I use his formal name in front of my parents. "What are you doing here?"

He opens his mouth to answer, but my mom cuts him off.

"Oh, he carried you to our house." I turn to her. "He saved your *life*," she smiles at Benjamin, warmly.

When I turn back to Ben, he looks embarrassed. I snap my head to my dad, to examine his expression and he's nodding in approval. I direct my gaze back to Ben, in wonder.

"*Thank you*, Benjamin," I breathe.

I try to imagine him, carrying my limp body, not knowing if I was dead or alive. It's a disturbing thought.

"You're welcome," he says, awkwardly, not liking the attention on him.

"Are you *hungry*, honey? You *must* be, you've been out since *Tuesday*." My mom informs me.

I tear my gaze away from Ben reluctantly, to face her again. "*What?* What's *today?*" I ask.

"Today's Thursday," she answers.

"*Oh*," my face falls. "I guess I am sorta hungry."

She nods. "Me and dad are going to go get you something from the cafeteria. What would you like to eat?"

The look my dad shoots her doesn't go unnoticed by me. She shoots him one of her own in return. I guess Ben still isn't *that* welcome yet, according to my dad of course.

"Umm, pasta?" I say, feeling my angry stomach come to life at the mention of it.

"Pasta it is!" She claps her hands together. "We'll be right back hun," she pats my knee. She gets up, forcing my dad to let go of my hand. He looks annoyed when she does. Suddenly, she pauses and leans down to kiss me on the forehead. "I'm so *glad* you're okay," she says, her voice getting thick with emotion.

"Me too," I breathe. "I love you, mom," I turn to my dad. "Dad," I add. The relief is transparent in my voice.

My dad smiles. "Love you too, kid."

"I love you *too*, honey," my mom smiles also, tears brimming in her eyes.

"Okay, okay, we all *love* each other. Now can we go get some *food?*" my dad teases, cracking a smile, his eyes crinkling in the corners.

Me and my mom laugh, then she leaves the room with my dad.

Ben watches me from a distance, making me feel uncomfortable. "This is *different*," I comment.

"What is?" he asks.

"*You, here*, with my parents," I raise my brows in disbelief.

"Oh," he smirks. "*That*."

"Yeah, *that*," I laugh. "Why are you standing so *far?* I'm not *contagious*," I joke. But then I suddenly become acutely aware that I have *no idea* what I look like right now.

Did I get burns from the lightning? It certainly *felt* like it.

Does my hair look like a homeless person's?

Do I even *have* hair?

I needed to find a mirror!

He laughs, almost uncomfortably. "No, you're not," he agrees. "I guess I just got freaked out by all of this. I thought...I thought you were going to *die*," he says, his face contorting in pain. I can tell the memory is still all too fresh in his mind.

I lose my breath for a moment, remembering the feeling myself. "Well, I *didn't*," I say finally. "I'm here and I'm here for a *reason*. I *have* to be, if I survived *that*."

He walks closer and sits down on my bed, watching me cautiously. "I'm glad you're here, love," he slowly reaches his hand up to gently brush my cheek. I breathe shallowly, savoring his touch.

I search his handsome face, getting lost in his perfect features for a moment. He looks much better now, his face is completely healed. He stares into my eyes with a curious expression.

"What is it, Ben?" I wonder aloud.

His eyebrows furrow. "It's just that...it's just that," he stutters.

My chest rises in panic. Oh no, maybe I *do* look awful?

Is my face covered in burns?

Or worse, *what if he wants to go back on what we decided to do?*

What if he's changed his mind about us? About *me?*

I wait, feeling more and more numb by the second. "*What?* What is it?" I ask, self-consciously.

"Your *eyes*," he says, looking at me strangely. "They're *green*."

I breathe a sigh of relief.

Is that all?

"My eyes are hazel, but they sometimes *look* green," I repeat the same phrase that I've been saying all my life.

"*No—*" Ben stops me. "Abby, your eyes are *really* green. They've changed *color*," he insists, staring at me with his own eyes wide. His expression is making me nervous.

"*What* are you *talking* about, Ben? Let me see, get me a mirror. There should be one in my mom's purse," I point to her purse, sitting on a chair.

He gets up, walks over to it and brings it to me. He sets it in my lap and I sit up as straight as I can. I unzip the purse with weak fingers and dig in it, searching for my mom's makeup bag. I pull it out, unzip it and find her mirror. I slowly lift it to my face. At first, I'm relieved to not see any burns or marks, but then quickly become alarmed when I find a stranger looking back at me in the mirror. I stare in shock, not recognizing my own reflection. Ben is right, my eyes *are* green. Not just a little hint of it, or flecks of it. My eyes have turned into a *whole* different color completely. A deep, dark, Emerald green. I gasp aloud, dropping the mirror. I glance back at Ben, who's watching me warily.

"*Oh my...what...why?* Is it *the curse*? What's *happening?*" I struggle, my breaths becoming shallow.

Inside, the panic is building.

Ben sits down, scooting closer to me. He takes my hands in his. "I don't *know*, Abby, but we're going to find out," he breathes. "It's going to be *okay*, I *promise*," he forces a strained smile. "I'm not going *anywhere*," he gives my hands a reassuring squeeze.

CHAPTER THIRTY
Dirty Work

* * *

"Are you *sure* you want to know?" Ben stares at me with guarded eyes.

"*Absolutely*," I nod. He looks like he's still deliberating whether or not he wants to tell me.

"Hey, you *promised*," I remind him.

He sighs. "I *know*. I'm just afraid it'll change how you *see* me..." he smiles nervously.

"*Really?* After *everything* we've been through lately? There's not much that would shock me now," I scoff.

We're sitting on Ben's front porch. It's been a week since I was in the hospital. My parents have slowly started letting me and Ben hang out. Right now, it's only in places they can watch us. I try to pretend that I don't notice my dad, who keeps finding reasons to work outside. Luckily, I recovered from my brush with death pretty well. I had to convince my parents that I've been wearing green contacts, though. I don't know how long I can drag *that* lie out for. I still haven't figured out the reason *why* my eyes changed color. Although, if I'm being perfectly honest with myself, I don't *want* to. I think Ben is afraid to look into it, also. I know that I'm going to need to face it eventually, but right now, I just need a break from any more drama.

He smirks. "Yeah, our lives have been *anything* but typical."

"Especially *yours*," I point out.

"*Okay*," he covers his face with his hands. "Ask away."

I pause and take a deep breath. "Who do you work for?" I feel my nerves building.

Ben lets out a breath before answering. "We work for *several* people. We don't have *one* boss. We're our *own* bosses. People come to *us* with an offer, and we either accept it or decline it. *If* we accept it, then we negotiate on a price."

Okay, I think. *So far, so good.*

The next question is harder. "What do you *do* on your jobs?"

"A lot of things...but they're all paid favors. For people who can't or *won't* take care of things *themselves*." I can hear him smiling from under his hands.

"*Illegal* things?" I assume, my pulse picking up.

He lifts his hands from his face but looks away, not wanting to meet my eyes. "....*Yes*..." he nods.

"So, you're *criminals?*" I feel my body grow cold.

He bites his lip, distracting me, then shrugs. "*Some* may look at us that way...I like to think of us more as...*repair* men."

"*Repair men?*" I repeat, my mouth drying up.

He looks at me now. "*Yeah,* if people have a problem or need something fixed, we *fix* it," he says simply.

"That's *disturbing*," I comment.

He pulls out a pack of cigarettes and a lighter from his pocket and slides a cigarette out, sticking it between his lips and lighting it. He furrows his eyebrows at me. "Are you *done* with the questions?"

"*Hardly.*"

I turn to see if my dad is watching us, but he's inside now.

I wonder if he's watching us from the window?

He's going to have *a lot* to say to me if he is. I don't think he supports the usage of tobacco, for underage people.

"What, *exactly*," I emphasize the word. "Do you *do?*" I notice he always seem to avoid the details.

He pauses. "Well, we all have our *'specialties'*, but we alternate sometimes..." he exhales smoke into the air, then continues, thoughtfully. "Max obviously takes the more *physical* jobs. Joseph is good at long stake outs and undercover jobs. Quinn is the best at stealing..." he trails off.

I feel nauseous.

"And you? What is your *'specialty'?*" I have to know.

"He's our *lucky charm.*" I hear a voice come from behind me.

I turn to see Max standing in the doorway.

"He can charm the pants off of *anyone*. Convince them to do just about *anything* he wants." Ben shoots Max a warning look. Max raises an instigating brow. "*Especially women*," he adds, laughing.

Ben cringes and I raise my eyebrows at him.

Has he been using this little *'skill'* on *me* the whole time? I *hope* not.

Max, sensing the trouble he's caused, adds suddenly, "*and* he's smart as hell, too. He can hack into any computer or bank account, and open any safe."

Ben shakes his head and stares at the ground, embarrassed.

"*Hey* Sparky, did I ever thank you for saving my baby brother's life?" Max changes the subject.

I sigh. "*Yes*, Max. You already thanked me. This is the *third* time now."

"Oh, okay. Just making sure," he smirks.

"Hey *Max*, could you maybe stop calling her *'Sparky'* now?" Ben interjects.

"Why?" Max accuses. Then his face dawns with realization. "*Oh...*"

I'm confused at first also, until a chill runs through my body as I understand what Ben means. My little nickname holds a whole new meaning, now.

How *odd* it is, that Max picked that particular nickname for me. Who would've *ever* guessed that I would've been struck by *lightning?*

"It's fine, Max. I don't mind it," I smile at him. He smirks at Ben like he won something. I turn back to Ben, wanting to pick up where we left off. "So, you *are* a con man?" I twist my lips. He looks back up at me.

"*Sorta*," he blushes.

I see my dad walk outside, from my peripheral vision and knock the cigarette out of Ben's mouth quickly. It bounces and falls to the ground.

"What was *that* for?" he accuses, his blue eyes wide. Max is laughing behind us.

"My *dad*," I point and Ben nods.

"So, you're going back to school tomorrow?" Ben asks. Max walks back into the house, sensing the entertainment is over for now.

"Yep," I answer.

The thought makes my stomach nervous. Word travels fast and now *everyone* knows me as *"the girl who got struck by lightning"*. Somehow, everyone found out about *Ben* being the one to carry me home also, which only added fuel to the fire about *'us'*. Meg had blown up my phone the days following the *'incident'*. I had to text and call her over and over again just to reassure her that I was *okay*. Riley made me FaceTime her to *prove* that I was okay. Even *Jamie* seemed to have gotten over our bad blood, and sent me flowers in the hospital. Ben was less than thrilled about that.

"Just stick to the story," he reassures me.

I nod. The story was, the lightning strike messed up my vision, causing me to need contacts. I just happened to pick green.

"What about *us?* What should I say about *that?*" I pry.

"That you're my girlfriend," he says, without missing a beat. I glance up at him, wanting to read his expression, to see if he's being serious. He takes my hands in his. "That's *if*, you'll have me," he smiles, shyly. My cheeks burn hot and my skin tingles.

"Are you doing that *charming* thing to me again? Are you using your *skill?*" I accuse him, disbelieving.

"I think *you're* the one who's charming *me*," he breathes, looking very much like he wants to kiss me.

"But what if...what if things *change,* Ben? What if...*I* change?" I stammer nervously, accidentally blurting out my fears.

He gulps. "It doesn't matter anymore. I can't away from you. I *won't*," he responds. His blue eyes look cloudy.

I feel a flash of heat run through my body and my skin prickles in the most *pleasant* way possible. My voice rasps, almost inaudibly. "Okay, then."

He leans forward, his eyes hooded. "So you *will* be my girlfriend?"

"*Yes*," I whisper, my heart thumping wildly.

"Do you want me to kiss you now?" he inches closer, his eyes on my lips.

"More than *anything*," I say huskily. The corners of his mouth pull up slightly, into a small smile.

"*AHEM!*" The sound of someone clearing their throat loudly startles us, and we both flinch back.

Ben lets go of my hands. I turn around and see my dad watching us. My face flames, the moment is ruined. I can't *believe* we got so caught up that I forgot my *dad* was watching.

"Maybe *later*, then," Ben smiles, mischievously. Then he pauses for a moment. "So...you're *okay* with my...*line of work?*" He raises his eyebrows at me.

I think for a moment. "You guys ever kill anyone?"

"Not yet," he smirks.

I gulp. "Then we're good, *for now.*"

CHAPTER THIRTY-ONE

Supernatural

I stand in the bathroom, fidgeting with my hair. I pull it up into a ponytail, then rip it back out, frustrated. My eyes look so noticeably *green* today, almost like they're *glowing*. I try putting on makeup, but it only seems to make them stand out *more*. I end up washing it all back off, scrubbing my face clean. I give up on my reflection at the same time that I hear the honk from outside. I grab my bag and jacket. On my way out, I pet Scout. I lock up my house and head outside. A thick fog hovers a few feet above the ground. I open the door to the SUV and climb in next to Ben. He smiles at me, grabbing my hand. He catches a glimpse of my eyes and swallows hard.

Max turns around in the driver's seat. "Hey Spark— *woah*..." he pauses.

Joseph and Quinn turn to stare at me also.

"It's *fine. Everything's* fine. There's *nothing wrong*," I grit my teeth down.

They shoot each other looks before turning away, looking anywhere but me.

There's an awkward silence on the way to school. I can't *believe* I'm riding with the Blake brothers now, I would've never imagined this happening when I first moved here. I never would've imagined that I'd be dating *Ben* either, though. I turn back towards him, and he's looking out the window. His lips are barely moving, silently singing the song on the radio. There's still so much that I don't *know* about him, I'm so impatient to find it all out.

We pull up to the school and all file out. I notice that people are staring and whispering as I take Ben's hand in mine and walk across the front lawn. Ben's brothers are flanking me on both sides. For some odd reason, I feel like *I* now have four body guards. People are even pointing, it's so *strange*. This time, I have to hear all the things people are saying about *me*.

"She got struck by lightning and lived, that's crazy."

"Benjamin is the one who saved her, he performed CPR on her, I heard she died for a few minutes before that."

"I heard they brainwashed her into their cult."

"I heard she's actually 'with' all of them."

I have to shake my head and laugh about that last one. As Ben and I walk down the hall together, Meg catches sight of me and smiles hugely. I wave at her and smile. A strange look crosses her face, like for a moment she almost doesn't recognize me. There's a static in the air as we enter the classroom, before we finally split up to take our seats.

At lunch I sit with Ben. I shift in my seat as Meg brings her tray over to join us. Ben looks alarmed as well. I know he's not exactly *great* at getting to know new people.

"*So*...I think it's time we formally met, now that you're *dating* my best friend," Meg says, decidedly. I smirk, entertained.

"I'm Meghan." She holds her hand out.

Ben looks at me and I raise my eyebrows at him pointedly. He concedes, and extends his hand out to her.

"Ben," he smiles.

"*Okay*... a man of few words. Gotcha," she says, vaguely disappointed.

Then she turns her attention back to me. "*Holy crap*, your *eyes!*" she notices, suddenly.

I feel a frisson of self-consciousness run through me. "I got contacts," I blurt out, immediately paranoid.

"*I'll say.* Where did you order *those* from? Those are awesome!" she grins.

Later at work, Jamie notices, too. I was relieved that he didn't have any visible scars or marks left from his fight with Ben.

"Did you get contacts?" he asks, after staring at me all night.

I drop a plate and it breaks. "*Sorry!*" I say, and start cleaning it up, immediately. "*Yes*, I did," I answer him anyway.

"Let me help you," he says, bending down to pick up some of the pieces. "They make you look *different*. The contacts, I mean..." he says, studying my face, closely.

"Yeah..." I let it drop, unsure if he meant it as a compliment or not. I cut my hand clumsily, on a piece of sharp porcelain. "Ah, *crap*," I complain.

It starts to bleed and Jamie glances up, looking alarmed. "Let me get you something for that."

I nod. But before he returns with a clean towel, I watch in amazement as the wound starts closing back up, by *itself*. A strange sound escapes my mouth. By the time Jamie returns with the towel, it's fully *healed*.

I hide my hand behind me. "I already got something for it, thanks Jamie. See you tomorrow," I blurt out, hurriedly, moving past him quickly. He stands with the towel in his hand and a confused look on his face. I search for Meg and grab her. "We gotta go."

I text Ben as soon as I get home.

Something's happened.

He returns my text almost instantly. *What is it?*

I felt too scared to even text it to him, so instead I tell him. *Meet me outside.*

I walk outside and Ben is waiting, he looks nervous. "What's going on?"

I hold out my hand to him. "*Look* at my hand, what do you see?"

He grabs it and turns it side to side, examining it. "*Nothing*," he shrugs.

"*Exactly*. I cut it on a piece of porcelain today at work, it was *bleeding* and everything and Jamie went—" I pause when I notice Ben's eyes briefly flash with anger at the mention of Jamie's name. Then I continue, more carefully. "He went to get me a towel and I watched it *heal* before my own eyes! It sealed *itself* back up!" My voice starts rising and my hands begin to shake.

Ben clasps both of his palms onto my upper arms, looking into my eyes. "Abby, *love*, calm down."

"*How* can I *calm down?*" I continue, rambling. "*Something* is *happening* to me, Ben. We need to *acknowledge* it."

"I *know*," he sighs, leaning forward and touching his forehead to mine. He lifts his hands up to cup my face in his hands. "You're right."

"I'm *scared.*" My eyes start to fill with tears.

"Me *too*," he admits, pulling me into his arms and holding me close. "But I'm going to help you figure this out, I *promise*." He embraces me in his arms, holding me tightly against his muscular chest. For a minute, I feel safe. I calm down a little bit, sighing deeply. He smells so good. When he lets go of me, he stares into my eyes.

"Do you think I'm becoming like her. Like...*Everly?*" I whisper.

Ben's eyes are wide and cautious, he takes my hands in his and stares down at them. "Let's hope not." My eyes drop to the ground. He lifts my chin up with his hand. "But I'm willing to be your guinea pig, if you want to try some stuff on me," he winks, trying to brighten my mood.

"Oh, *really?* Like *what?*" My lips twitch.

"*Well*," he stares at my lips. "First we should probably make sure that I won't turn into a frog if you *kiss* me," he smirks.

"Maybe you'll turn into a *prince?*" I raise my brows at him.

He pulls me back into his arms, pressing me flush against his body. "*Highly* doubtful," he murmurs against my lips, before pressing his lips softly against mine.

I reciprocate, letting myself get lost for a moment. When he pulls away, I feel dizzy.

"Think I've got something," he raises his eyebrows.

"What?" I ask, too love-drunk to think clearly.

"Your eyes seem to glow more when I kiss you," he points out.

"Ha-ha, very funny," I say, sarcastically.

"No, *seriously*," he smiles. "Look for yourself."

I sigh and pull my phone out of my back pocket, putting on the camera. He's right, my eyes *are* glowing brighter. Like this morning, when I was getting ready.

I wonder what's the connection?

"*Ben!*" I hear Max call from their front porch. We both turn. "*We got a job!*" he yells.

I watch as all of the other brothers load into the SUV. Worry settles into my stomach and my eyes snap to Ben's. He shrugs. "Duty calls. I'll text you later."

I open my mouth to object, but he's already ran off and is climbing into the SUV. I watch them as they pull out of the driveway and drive off.

"Be careful," I say to myself.

I walk back inside and into my room. I lie on my bed and start texting Riley. I look over and notice that the rose that Ben gave me, in the window sill, finally wilted. I get the feeling a lot of more strange things are to come.

CHAPTER THIRTY-TWO
Amateur

I stay up late waiting for Ben's text. Sometime during the waiting, I fall asleep. My phone buzzes against my hand, waking me up. I glance at it.

I'm home. It says simply.

I check the time, it's 3:47 a.m. I sigh and roll back over.

What were they doing that could possibly take that *long?*

I wake up later that morning feeling grouchy after getting little sleep. I groggily get ready for school. I wait for Ben and his brothers to honk at 7:40, like they usually do. But at 7:50, I start to wonder if they're coming. I lock up the house and walk over to theirs, to knock at their door. When I get no answer, I try calling Ben. Again no answer. I sigh in frustration and run to get my bike. I don't want to be late with no note *twice*. They'd definitely call my parents *this* time. I pedal hard, more bitter than ever that I still don't have my license or a car. I get to class right as soon as the bell rings, with my hair stuck to my sweaty forehead.

At lunch, Ben still isn't at school yet. I know he made it home safely, but I wondered if everything went okay? A disturbing thought flashes through my mind.

What if he's hurt again?
What if something bad happened?

But knowing it'll drive me crazy if I keep thinking that way, I drive those thoughts out of my mind. I decide that maybe I should text him again.

Where are you? Is everything okay?

Meg walks up and nudges me with her elbow. "You sitting with me today?" she smiles.

"Yeah," I say, distractedly.

"Well, don't sound so *excited* about it," she teases.

"Sorry," I laugh and try to fix a pleasant look onto my face.

We go through the line to get out food. I start walking with my tray, but two girls suddenly move in front of me, blocking my way. I try to go around them, but they move as I do, mirroring my actions. I realize that I *recognize* them. They're the same two trashy girls that were sitting with Ben at lunch that one time.

"Excuse me," I say, semi-politely.

"Where are you going? Looking for *Ben?*" The blonde one smiles.

I stare at her, my irritation growing. Meg, who was walking in front of me, has turned around and is watching me from behind their heads.

"No. Now move out of my way," I demand.

"Well, it's a good thing you weren't looking for Ben...since *we* were with him all night." The raven-haired girl smiles, slyly. Then she adds, "he's probably pretty *tired*," she winks. They look at each other and giggle.

For a second, ice-water runs through my veins and my heart drops into my stomach. Then I realize that they're bluffing. They're jealous that Ben isn't interested anymore. They must've heard that we were dating and about Ben saving my life.

I sigh, trying not to slap one of them in the face, which is exactly what I *want* to do. "I don't have the patience to deal with any of Ben's ex-*groupies* right now."

Both of their smiles slide off of their faces. "Did you just call us *groupies?*" The blonde one bites out, angrily.

I shrug and try to move around them again, but the raven-haired one shoves my shoulder. "What makes you think *you're* so *special?* What makes you think that *you* won't be his *next* ex? You think he won't *throw you away* once he's done with *you?*" she fumes, bitterness leaking into her voice. People are starting to turn and stare. We're causing a commotion.

Great, that's all I need, I think.

"*Move* out of my way," I repeat.

The tray starts to tremble in my hands. Panicked, I turn and start walking in the other direction. The raven-haired girl grabs my shoulder, yanking me back.I almost drop my tray.

"Don't *touch* me!" I snap and turn back around.

"Hey!" Meg finally pipes up. "Leave her alone!" she attempts to defend me.

The raven-haired girl pushes her back though, muscling her out of the way. "You stay out of this."

Meg looks effectively frightened and reluctantly does as she says.

Then they move on either side of me, cornering me, trapping me. The blonde one knocks the tray out of my hands, spilling its contents onto my clothes. They both point and laugh.

Everyone is staring now.

For some reason, I can't find a *single* teacher. I feel like I'm going to cry, so I dart away, but they corner me again.

"I don't think she's *tough* enough for Ben, anyway. What are you going to *do* about it, *new girl?*" The raven-haired one sneers.

Something inexplicable builds inside of me, a strange vibration starting from my toes, traveling all the way to the top of my head. I can't control it or slow it down. The sensation fills my body, threatening to bubble over. But for some reason, my mind is completely numb, void of thoughts.

"I said, *MOVE!*" I yell.

The vibration ceases, freeing me of its hold. Both of the girls go flying abruptly backwards, as if they were yanked by the *air* itself. The blonde one smacks into someone walking with their tray, knocking them and its contents over. The raven-haired girl lands on a table, her eyes wide with alarm.

A hush falls over the cafeteria, as pretty much all of the tenth grade stares at me. Meg walks over to me, cautiously. "What did you *do* to them?" she asks in a low voice, with fear in her eyes.

"*I* didn't do *anything*." I hold my hands up in surrender.

Some boy sitting close by, yells out. "What *are* you?" he accuses.

Suddenly, I feel incredibly isolated. My body grows cold with fear.

I stand speechless and unmoving, until someone grabs me by the arm.

It's Ben.

I didn't see him come in. *Did he see the whole thing?*

"Come *on*, Abby," he urges, his eyes alarmed. "We need to get you out of here."

I let him practically drag me from the cafeteria, into the school parking lot. We approach the SUV.

"Get in," he orders, before hopping into the driver's seat, himself.

I do as he says, even though I'm aware that I left all of my stuff *and* my bike behind at school. He backs out swiftly and rides away from the school.

I'm guessing he'll pick up his brothers later?

Hopefully they won't be mad. I don't even know what to say to him, I don't know what he *saw*. But I assume that he saw enough to instinctively get me far away from the school.

I watch him drive, not knowing where we're going. I know we're not going home because he passed the street that our houses are on. He looks more stressed than usual. His hair is messy, like he's been running his hands through it non-stop. His eyes have bags under them and he's hunched over the wheel like he's been driving for hours. I wait for him to say something, but he seems to be in his own head. I get too impatient and decide to speak up first.

"Ben, where are we going?" I ask, carefully.

"Somewhere *safe*," he replies, keeping his eyes on the road.

"What about *school?* They'll call my parents," I worry.

He turns to me. "Abby, you *can't* go back to school," he says, his eyes serious.

"Until *tomorrow?*" I ask, naïvely.

His mouth sets into a flat line. "Let me rephrase that, you can't go back to *that* school."

My brows furrow. "Why *not?*"

He sighs. "It's not *safe* for you anymore."

I get mad suddenly. "*Why not?* Are you afraid your little *'girlfriends'* are going to try to beat me up again?" I fume.

"No, I'm afraid that *you'll* hurt someone and they'll take you away."

Oh...*right.*

I gulp. "Who's *'they'?*"

He sighs in frustration. "I don't *know*, Abby...the FBI, the government. Whoever would know what to *do* with a teenage girl who possesses powers strong enough to hurt *a lot* of people."

"*Powers?*" I scrunch up my face. "Is *that* what you think that was?"

"I *know* that's what it was," he says, emphatically.

"*How?*" I ask, in denial.

"Because I was *there*, Abby. I *watched* you, myself. I *know* because I've never seen anything *like* that before. And either has anyone *else* in that room.

What happened today, will *not* go unheard of. It'll spread from the students to the teachers, and from the teachers to the parents. Pretty soon *everyone* will know and they'll want answers. Are *you* going to be able answer them?"

I pause and shake my head. How can I begin to explain what *I* don't even understand?

"I didn't know you were there. You weren't at school all morning," I try to hide the disappointment in my voice. My cheeks flush with embarrassment at the thought of him watching the whole ordeal unfold.

"I *know*. I'm *sorry*. None of us woke up on time. We were all out late last night."

I raise my eyebrows, recalling what those girls in the cafeteria had said to me. "Were you just out working?" I ask.

He looks at me, bemused. "Yeah, I told you that. *Why?*"

I twist my lips. "Those girls said you were with *them* last night."

His eyes widen and he swallows. "Well, I *wasn't*." He pauses and seems to think for a moment. "Is *that* what that whole fight was about?" he asks and I nod. "Well, I guess I have *two* things to apologize for then," he says, shaking his head. "I'm sorry they were bothering you. Even though, I'm sure they won't be bothering you *again*," he smirks, proudly.

"It's okay," I sigh. "But I didn't mean to *hurt* them," I clarify.

I've never felt like I couldn't control my own actions, until now. I didn't know if there was anything *scarier* than that. I didn't want to hurt anyone else. Especially those I love or care about. There was no easy solution to this, nothing to ease my worry.

Ben looks at me. "I know," he reassures me.

Then I ask the bolder question. "Were you really *with* both of them?"

He swallows, nervously and keeps his eyes on the road this time. "Not at the *same* time. But *yes*, I casually dated both of them...at *different* times."

I know I shouldn't, but I still feel hurt. "*Why?*" I have to ask.

"I may be cursed, but I'm still a *guy*," he shrugs, smirking irresistibly.

"Oh..." I let it drop. I don't like the images running through my head.

There's an awkward silence, before Ben speaks up again. "I picked girls I *knew* I wouldn't fall for. I didn't want anyone to get *really* hurt," he explains.

That made sense, sort of. "Sounds like *you* were afraid to get hurt, too," I guess out loud.

"Not as afraid as I am *now*," he smirks and reaches over to squeeze my hand.

What does that mean?

He's falling in love with me?

Or he's afraid of me now, after what he just saw me do today in the cafeteria?

Since I'm too afraid to ask any of *those* questions, I just smile back.

CHAPTER THIRTY-THREE
Confessions

We wind through the forest until we come upon an abandoned garage. I glance over at Ben, but he offers no explanation. He reaches up and hits a button on his visor that I never noticed before. The garage opens and we park inside.

"Why are we here?" I ask, finally.

"I told you," he smiles at me.

"*This* is the safe place?" I look out the windows.

"Safe enough," he shrugs.

We get out and I immediately notice this isn't just a parking garage.

It's a thief's paradise.

I recognize the red Lamborghini parked beside us, along with a few more shiny, expensive vehicles. Ben walks around the SUV to stand beside me.

"*Woah*," I breathe. "So this is where you *store* everything?" I turn to glare at him. He shrugs, noncommittal and smirking.

"Can I *pick* one?" I ask, joking.

He laughs. "You don't have a *license* yet."

I scoff. "Oh and driving without a license is more serious of an offense than vehicle theft, assault, trespassing, fraud, extortion, illegal possession of a firearm—"

"How did you know we own guns?" he accuses.

"Are you forgetting that I already saw you with one, that day you rescued me from that wolf? I can only assume that you have *more* at your house...?"

He laughs. "Well, *yes*. But they're only for *emergencies*. We have to be able to *defend* ourselves. We're really just a bunch of unsupervised teenagers, after all," he smirks, pleased with his explanation.

"Yeah, I don't think you guys need *guns* at all for that. I've *seen* you in action, *remember?* I can only assume that your *brothers* taught you how to fight?" I raise a brow, fighting a smile.

"You *assume* correctly," he smiles back.

"Anyway, me driving would *much* less of an offense than all of those other laws you that and your brothers have undoubtedly broken," I finish my point.

"You forgot one."

"What did I forget?"

"Underage use of alcohol and tobacco," he smirks.

I throw my hands up. "*Again, not* the worst one!"

He laughs. I make my way over to the red Lambo and he follows behind me silently.

"Can I see the inside?" I ask, feeling like a little kid.

"Oh, why not," he grins.

He walks over to a wall and picks the right key. He unlocks it as he walks over, the vehicle's lights responding accordingly, as they open like eyes. I look up at him for a moment, my eyes asking permission to get in and he nods, smiling, looking entertained. I open the strange door, feeling a lot like I'm in the movie *Back to the Future*. I climb inside, and am immediately overwhelmed by the scent of fresh leather. There are so many buttons and gadgets inside, it's like some sort of spaceship. Ben opens the door and climbs in also. He sits beside me.

"This one's my favorite," he smiles, looking like a young boy for a moment. "Too bad we have to deliver it soon."

Not wanting to ask for more information, I just nod. He reaches over suddenly startling me, but I relax when I realize that he's just starting the car. He presses a button and the engine roars to life, all of the buttons lighting up inside.

"Pretty cool, huh?" he smiles.

"Yeah," I breathe. "I can't believe you got to *drive* this thing," I confess.

He nods, not being able to wipe the smile fully off of his face. I've never seen him look so happy.

Boys and their toys, I think.

We sit, listening to the radio for a few minutes.

"Ben..." I say, hesitantly.

He turns and gazes at me. "*Yes?*"

"What do you think is going to happen *now?* I mean, I can't go back to school," I cringe.

He sighs. "Well, maybe you can *change* schools? Portland *is* a big city, there are plenty of schools to choose from."

"You're right," I sigh. "Guess I'll have to make something up to my parents," I say.

"Just say you're being bullied," he shrugs.

I nod. It *would* make sense, with me being new and all.

"There's something *else*, Ben...."

"*What* else?" he asks, alarmed by the tone of my voice.

"Well, it's just a theory, but it would mean good news for you and your family," I start.

His brows furrow. "And that *is?*"

"Well...I *think* I may have broken the curse on you and your family," I try to sound as hopeful as I feel.

"What makes you think *that?*" he asks, looking skeptical.

"You know that rose you left for me a long time ago? How I've kept it ever since?"

He nods, looking embarrassed.

"It *died*," I say, simply.

He looks confused. "*And?*"

"Well, it was alive for over a month. Roses don't usually live that long, not after they've been *cut* and put into simple vases with water. It *never* wilted or lost a petal or a leaf. And I know this sounds *weird*, but I swear sometimes it would almost *glow*."

He laughs, shrugging. "Maybe you just have a green thumb," he suggests.

"*No*, Ben. After my eyes changed, you know? After I got struck by lightning. I came home and it was *dead* all of a sudden. Shriveled up and wilted. I know it sounds crazy, but I think it was a symbol of the curse and after I *broke* it, the rose died."

He waits a moment and lets it sink in. "Well, that does *sound* crazy. But if you think it's true, *well*, I guess I have no other choice than to... *believe* you," he decided. He smiles at me, breathless and his eyes wide with wonder. I smile back, hesitantly.

"Do you want to...test it out?" His eyes twinkle.

"What do you mean?" My heart starts to race.

"Well..." he reaches over, placing his hand on my thigh. My skin tingles where it rests. "If *nothing* is keeping us *apart* anymore..." he whispers, his eyes turning that cloudy, blue color again. He starts to lean into me.

I feel too hot suddenly, but I manage to force my voice out. "Well, I'm not *entirely* sure that *nothing* is keeping us apart," I blurt out.

He stills. "But you said you think the curse was broken?" he narrows his eyes at me.

"Well, I think I more like...*transferred* it?" I say, carefully.

He looks confused again.

"What I mean is, when I *broke* it, I think the *old* curse went back into effect... The one that was on *my* family."

His eyes widen a little.

"Maybe this *whole* time it wasn't about *your* family being cursed, it was about *mine*," I reach. "Think about it, Everly couldn't have just turned into a witch for nothing. She was *always* one, but never used her powers. Or never knew she *had* them, until that day with Cillian."

"Then *why* have there not been more witches in your family *since* then?" he asks, looking more lost by the minute.

I twist my lips. "Because the curse was on *your* family for so long? I'm not sure about that part either..." I hesitate. "But I *can* tell you for sure, the curse is no longer on *your* family anymore." I pause and take a deep breath. "And Everly's powers have been transferred to *me...indefinitely.* I'm literally your worst nightmare now," I laugh, really wanting to cry. "I'm," I suck in a shaky breath, trying not to lose my courage. *"A witch,"* I finally admit. I *finally* said the word out loud. I feel like a weight has been lifted off of my shoulders.

Ben just stares at me, absorbing everything. It feels like for too long. I start to panic inside, waiting for him to speak.

He's going to tell me to leave him alone, to stay away from his family, once and for all.

Tears build in my eyes.

"It's *okay—*" I start.

"Wait," he stops me. *"I...I knew* that...already, Abby. I figured it out. Not *everything* you said, but I had an *idea,* after all of the strange things that have *happened* to you. I've been trying to find a way to *change* it. It's *my* fault that this has *happened* to you," he hangs his head in shame. His voice gets abruptly thick with emotion. "I should just have stayed *away* from you. I should've *listened* to my brothers. I knew better than to drag you into all of this. And when you told me you were going to try to *break* the curse, I shouldn't have *let* you. I should've *stopped* you," he shakes his head in despair, regret filling his voice. "I was *selfish* and I'm *sorry,*" he says into his chest. "I just wanted a *real* chance with you. I wanted to know what it felt like..."

"What *what* felt like?" I whisper.

He looks up at me. *"Love."*

My breath catches in my throat and my body feels warm all over.

"I *love* you, Abby, and I don't care *what* you are," Ben says softly.

His blue eyes are clear and honest. My heart is beating as fast as a hummingbird's wings. I feel like I've been set free of all restraints.

"I love you, *too*," I whisper in wonder, an unbreakable smile spreading across my face. His eyes light up even more.

He smirks back at me. "At least we have *one* thing figured out."

He leans forward and *this* time, I don't stop him. His lips meet with mine in fervent passion. Then his lips trail down to my jawline in feather-light kisses. My breathing becomes heavy, labored. His kisses lower to my neck, and then my collarbone. I feel like I need to hold on to something. That's when I remember that Benjamin Blake had yet *another* side to him that I'd never seen, although I'd *heard* about it.

"What the *bloody hell* are you two *doing* in there?" Someone yells, startling us both.

We both turn to see Max staring down at us through the window of the Lambo. His arms are crossed in disapproval. Ben moves away from me and sighs. Joseph and Quinn are standing a few feet behind Max, laughing.

"*Benjamin*, get the *hell* out of the Lamborghini!" Max demands. Ben smirks at me, then does as his brother says.

"You *too*, Sparky," he points at me through the window.

My face flames and I smooth my hair, before I step out.

CHAPTER THIRTY-FOUR
Safe

"How'd you get here?" Ben asks Max, scratching his neck.

"We found a way," Max smirks. "Word spread around school pretty fast. I thought this was where you'd be."

I shuffle my feet, uncomfortably. "So, you *know* what happened?" I ask.

Max shakes his head, laughing bitterly. "I think you caused more of a stir, than when Benjie boy got into that fight."

My throat gets dry at the thought. "I guess Ben was right that I can't return to Portland High, then?"

"Not unless you want to be burned at the stake," Max Jokes.

I pale.

Ben shoots Max a look.

"She knows I'm *joking*," Max laughs. "The more important question is, what were you two *doing* in that Lambo?" Max raises his brows, inquisitively. Joseph and Quinn snicker.

I stare at the ground. Ben fights a smile.

"She wanted to see the inside of it, so I was showing her," he shrugs.

"I'm *sure* you were," Max's voice drips with implication.

My phone buzzes in my pocket, breaking the awkward moment.

Crap, it's my mom! I let it go to voice mail.

"Who was that?" Ben asks.

I sigh. "My mom."

A few beats later my phone buzzes again with a text message.

Where are you? The school called and said you left. They also said some sort of incident occurred at school today and now two girls are hurt? CALL ME ASAP.

Double crap.

"I need to get home," I say.

Ben nods. "I'll take you."

"The *hell* you will!" Max laughs. "Not by *yourself!*"

"Since when do *you* care?" Ben scoffs.

"Since I realized that *she's* more dangerous than *us*," he laughs harder, shaking his head again.

I twist my lips and try not to smile.

More dangerous than *that* group of lugs? I found *that* hard to believe.

Ben looks surprised.

Max walks by him and claps him on the back. "Give me the keys," he demands, holding out his hand.

Ben sighs, producing them from his pocket and dropping them into Max's palm. "Joseph, Quinn, stay here. I'll be right back." They both nod.

Max gets into the SUV, Ben gets in the passenger seat and I climb into the back. The ride back to my house feels like forever. I don't know if my mom or dad will be home yet. They usually work until five, or sometimes later. But I'm worried that one or *both* of them will be waiting up on me *today*. Just as I'm thinking about it, my dad texts me.

Where are you? Your mom is worried.

I feel butterflies in my stomach. I hope I can pull this off, my parents don't *ever* need to know the truth. I feel bad to leave them worrying, so I text him back.

I'm on my way home.

I sigh and sit back in my seat, looking out the window. Meg hasn't texted me all day, either has Jamie about missing work. It makes my stomach nervous. *Usually* when you miss work without calling, your boss calls *you*. It makes me think that something's wrong.

Maybe Jamie *knows...*?

Unless Meg made up a lie for me?

Would she *do* that?

Does she still even trust me as her friend?

Even after my unexplainable behavior today in the cafeteria?

I would really hate to not ever talk to her again, we've become close. I'm closer to her than I am to Riley now.

What would *Riley* think of all this madness?

She'd probably think I was crazy. My phone buzzes again and my heart falls into my stomach with worry. But then my whole body warms when I notice that it's a text from *Ben*. I look up and see him smirking from the front seat.

Wish I was sitting back there with you ;)

For a moment, I forget about all of my problems. I smile like a schoolgirl.

Me too. I text him back.

FYI...the Lamborghini is definitely my favorite now... He texts me.

I feel myself blushing and am too shy to look up to see if Ben is watching me.

"We're here," Max says, interrupting my thoughts.

I look up to see that we're in front of my house, Max has pulled the SUV up to the curb.

I clear my throat. "Thanks," I say to both of them. "Wish me *luck*," I add.

"*Good luck*," Max says.

I hop out of the SUV, shutting the door behind me. I hear it pull away and I start to make my way to my front door.

"*Abby*," I hear Ben's voice from behind me.

I flinch, whirling around. "I thought you *left!* You *scared* me," I laugh, breathless.

"Sorry," he smirks. "I told Max I needed to make sure you were okay."

I smirk back. "Surprised he *let* you."

"Me too," he laughs and I love the way it sounds, like a soothing song to my ears.

"Well, I'm okay," I shrug.

"I know," he smiles.

"Then *why?*" I start.

"For *this*," he smiles, pulling me by the waist towards him.

"This is *different* side of you," I mumble, checking to see if anyone is looking.

"You haven't seen *anything* yet," he waggles his eyebrows at me.

I giggle in disbelief at the dramatic change in our relationship. Just as quickly as he was being playful, his mood abruptly shifts. He wraps his arms tightly around my waist, then drags them slowly up my sides, all the way up to my arms. All the while, staring into my eyes with intensity. I'm already struggling to breathe correctly, even though he's *barely* touched me. He lifts his hands and cradles my face between them, gently. His eyes are so deceptively innocent and hypnotizing. Ironically, he chooses that moment to notice mine, too.

"You must like this..." he murmurs, smiling faintly.

"*Why?*" I have to clear my throat, because my voice cracks, much to my embarrassment. "Why do you say that?" I finish.

He brushes his thumb against my lips, making me melt inside. "Your eyes are glowing again."

I feel myself shrinking back. "I'm sorry, do they scare you?" I whisper, looking down, trying to hide them.

He lifts my chin, forcing me to meet his eyes. "No, I *like* it. They help me understand how you feel."

I smirk. "*Okay.*"

"*Plus*, they look pretty cool," he smiles.

I laugh.

"I like *that*, too," he adds.

"*What?*" I ask.

"Your laugh," he smiles.

I feel a thrill run through me. "You're being *sweet* today," I breathe.

"What can I say? I think you bring it out in me," he smiles, his eyes on my lips.

Then he kisses me softly, running his hands through my hair. My knees get weak, so I wrap my arms around his neck, leaning into him, trying to hold myself up. When we both can't breathe anymore, he releases me and holds me in his arms. I rest my head on his chest and listen to his heart, it's racing as fast as mine is. He smells amazing as usual, peculiar that he never *smells* like cigarettes even though he smokes.

"*Abigail,*" I hear my dad's voice, coming from behind me. A shock runs through me, I turn around to see him and my mom, pulled up to the curb, in the truck. Ben lets go of me. "*Get inside,*" my dad demands. He looks *beyond* pissed. My mom watches me, with a stern look on her face, also.

"...I'd better *go*," I mumble.

"Yeah," Ben nods. "Let me know how it goes," he runs a hand through his hair.

"I will," I promise.

I walk up my driveway, following my parents. I take one last look at Ben, watching him as he walks to his house. Then I sigh and prepare for the lecture of a lifetime.

CHAPTER THIRTY-FIVE
Bad News

"Why was *Benjamin* here?" My dad questions me, whirling around on me the moment the front door shuts. But before I can respond, he's already asking another question. "Is *that* who you left school with? Did *he* get you to skip?" he fumes.

"I wasn't trying to *skip*, dad," I sigh. "I *left*...for another reason..."

My mom who's standing beside him, cuts in. "Was it about those girls?"

He turns to her. "*What* girls?"

I maintain eye contact with her, too afraid to look at my dad. "Yes, it had to do with them," I confirm.

"Were they trying to *fight* you?" She asks, with a look of horror on her face.

"*What girls*?" My dad repeats.

My mom waves him off. "I'll tell you later," she mumbles.

"Yes," I confess. "They started a fight with me at lunch. They wouldn't let me sit down and when I tried, they knocked my tray onto my clothes." I looked down at the dried stains on my clothes, suddenly remembering that I needed to change.

My dad looks surprised and my mom looks worried. "Well, did you go to the principal's office and *tell* them what happened?" she asks.

"...Well, *no*..." I mumble.

"Did they *hit* you?" My mom comes over to me and starts inspecting me for injuries.

I remember what Ben said, that I *couldn't* go back. I had to pretend that the bullying had gotten out of hand. Even though, deep down, I was aware that I could probably win *any* fight right now.

"*No*," I laugh awkwardly. "But if I go *back,* they probably will. I've...been meaning to *tell* you, mom," I stare at my hands, feigning embarrassment. "I've been having problems with the girls at school for a *while* now..."

Her eyes grow wider. "*Really*? Oh, *honey*. I thought things were going so *well*?" She takes my hands in hers, sympathetically.

My dad shuffles on his feet uncomfortably, looking an awful like he regrets his initial accusations.

"Yeah, not *really*..." I laugh again, awkwardly. At least that's not *totally* untrue.

My dad steps in suddenly, and my mom lets go of my hands. "Well, I'm *sorry* to hear that, baby girl. But me and your mom have been *talking*," he puts his arm around her. "And well, we think that maybe the trouble isn't *you*... maybe it's that boy you've been hanging around."

"*Ben*. You know his name, dad," I say, irritated. "We've had this conversation before. Ben *isn't* a bad influence on me. He *saved* me, *remember?*"

He sighs. "Of *course* I do. It's just that we can't help but think that he brings you... well, *trouble*. You never *used* to have problems at school before. Also, the whole lightning strike incident was a little...*strange*, to say the *least!* I can't put my finger on it, but there's just something not *right* about him."

I wish I could be angrier, but I'm more frightened about how unexpectedly *perceptive* my dad has been.

I look at my mom. "Is this how *you* feel, too? Or is it just dad?" I ask, tears threatening to spill from my eyes.

My mom's mouth turns into a flat line, she looks at my dad and he nods at her. She turns back to me. "I'm afraid your father's *right*, you've been acting *different* since we moved here."

If only they knew the real reasons, I think.

"I'm *growing up!*" I throw my hands up, in frustration. "If that's what you're mistaking for *bad behavior*, I'm just growing up!" I plead.

My dad shakes his head. "We *realize* that. That's why me and your mom have been *thinking*...well, we want to move *back* to Pemberton. We think it'd be best for *you*. To be back home, with all the friends you grew up with. It's a smaller, *safer* school. Me and mom could *easily* find work again with all the connections we have."

His voice seems to be getting smaller as he speaks, either that or my brain is trying to block out his words. Dread spreads throughout my body. The picture my dad is painting in his head, must look all sunshine and roses to *him*. But to *me*, it's all storm clouds and rain.

"Wha-what? *Why?*" I ask, completely flabbergasted.

My dad makes a face. "I already *told* you, baby girl. We don't think this is the *place* for you."

"I don't *want* to move. I just want to change schools," I clarify.

"The decision's already been *made*." My dad says, in a stern voice.

My heart sinks into my stomach. My eyes snap to my mom's. "Mom, *say* something!" I plead.

"I'm *sorry* honey, you know your father, always so *set* in his ways." She shakes her head.

I feel betrayed. I can't *believe* they're being this dramatic. I *can't* move back. Not after everything that's *happened*. I can't leave *Ben*.

I *won't*.

Angry tears build in my eyes. "I'm *not* moving," I cross my arms.

My dad starts turning red, then he steps forward, closer to me. "*You* will *do as we say*, we're *your parents*," he yells at me, pointing in my face.

I start to feel the numbness taking over, the vibration starting at my feet. I look down and the floor is vibrating, slightly. My parents are too distracted by our argument to notice. A flash of fear shoots through me.

I need to get away from them. *Now*.

"Do you *understand?*" My dad mistakes my silence for rebellion and grows impatient.

I grit my teeth down. "*Yes*."

I try to control the vibration from spreading, holding it in with all my might.

"Honey, we *really* just want what's *best* for you. We're your *parents*, we *love* you." My mom tries to reassure me.

I want to tell her that I love her, too, but the vibration has a hold on me, spreading its numbness throughout me. It imprisons my emotions. I feel it tingling its way up my legs. I know I have to get away now. *Fast*. It's climbing and that's *bad*.

"Okay," I manage.

I'm petrified to move or say anything more. My dad mistakes my abruptness for sarcasm and gets more upset with me.

"Go to your *room,* young lady!" he commands.

Gladly, I think.

I start to turn, stiffly.

"Wait," he says.

I turn back slowly, dreading facing him.

"Your *phone?*" he holds out his hand expectantly, palm facing upward.

I stiffly take my phone out of my pocket and drop it into his hand.

I feel the vibration working its way up my torso. My dad looks at me strangely. I turn quickly and walk briskly down the hall. I pass Scout in the hall, she cowers against the wall when she sees me pass. I turn the doorknob and slide into my room. I shut the door and press against it. It vibrates, shaking the walls. Startled, I jump off of it. I pace my room, not knowing how to *control* it. I needed to figure out a way to reign it in. Unfortunately, the panic of the thought of leaving Ben is weighing heavily on my mind.

I *can't* leave him, he's the *only* one who understands me, the only one I can *talk* to. Not to mention, I *love* him....and he loves *me*.

I still can't *believe* he said it.

I can't believe I'm that *lucky*.

The vibration has worked its way up my arms. I lie face down in my bed, trying to smash it down. But it doesn't slow. Instead, it works its way from my shoulders, up to my neck, and then to my head. My bed starts to shake. I grab my pillow and scream into it.

"*STOP!*"

I feel the force rip out of my body. I hear a strange popping noise throughout the house, before the lights go out, leaving me lying in the dark. I sit up in my bed, alarmed. I hear my parents in the living room, freaking out. I must've cut out the lights in the entire house. Scout is barking. I sigh.

I needed to figure out this whole *"powers"* thing, it was getting really annoying.

The exact thing that I was afraid of, is happening.

*I almost hurt my parents...*I let that sink in.

I *am* dangerous to them.

If they make me upset and I can't *control* it, or get away *fast* enough, I could *hurt* them. I would *never* forgive myself if that happened. I had to stay away from them until I learned how to control it. There's *no* way I can move back to Minnesota now.

I need to talk to Ben, he's the only one who can help me figure this out.

CHAPTER THIRTY-SIX
Runaways

"Are you *okay*, honey?" My mom pokes her head in my room.

She's holding a flashlight in her hand, and she shines it my way.

"Yeah, mom. I'm okay." I hold up my hand, shielding my eyes from the bright light.

She sits on my bed beside me. "That was so *strange*. The lights went out for no reason. *All of them!*"

"What do you think happened?" I ask, just wanting to hear a reasonable answer come out of her mouth.

"I don't know, but your father's on the phone with the electric company, so I guess we'll get it figured out," she sighs.

"In the meantime, here's a flashlight." She hands me another flashlight that I didn't notice she was holding. I take it from her and she stares strangely at me for a moment. "When are you going to stop wearing those *green* contacts? I miss *your* beautiful eyes," she says, tucking my hair behind my ear.

It makes me a little sad, she misses her *daughter*. Who I was before we moved here. When I was *normal*.

"I don't *know*, mom. I really like them," I raise my eyebrows at her.

She sighs. "Okay well, if *you* like them, I *guess* they're fine," she says, reluctantly. She sits on my bed for a moment, quietly. "I'm sorry about your *father*," she says suddenly, surprising me. I wait. "He can be *very* stubborn. I know...I know you like *Benjamin*," she confesses. Embarrassment washes over me. "Truthfully, I don't think he's that *bad*," she looks over at me, her eyes apologetic. I remain silent, not knowing what to say. "To be honest, I was really starting to *like* it here. I don't really want to move back, either," she admits.

I feel a flicker of hope spark inside of me.

"Do you think you can convince dad to *stay?*" I ask hopefully.

"I could *try*," she shrugs. "But I'm not too convinced that it would *work*," she admits.

"Thanks, mom," I smile and hug her.

"You're welcome, honey. Just...*don't* get your hopes up, okay?" she warns.

I nod.

Then she kisses me on the forehead. "Now get some rest."

I watch her as she walks away, but then I remember. "*Mom?*"

"Yes?" She turns around.

"Do I still have to go to school tomorrow?" I wonder.

"Not tomorrow, honey. Me and dad have to figure this all out," she sighs, sounding exhausted about it.

"Okay," I nod, thankful.

I was dreading seeing any of *those* faces again.

My mom forces a strained smile, then closes the door to my room behind her.

* * *

I wake up early the next day, to the sound of my phone vibrating next to my face. I squint my eyes open, confounded. Then I spy my phone, resting on my pillow. My mom must've got it from my dad and put it there for me early this morning when she went to work.

I slide over the screen, noting the time, it reads 8:15 a.m. When I see how many messages I've missed, I'm instantly alarmed. The first message is from last night. It's from Meg, I feel my stomach churn nervously as I open it.

I told Jamie you were sick, but I'm sure he'll hear about what happened soon. Everyone's talking about it, Abbs. I don't think you should come to school tomorrow. Somebody took a video, and now it's all over the internet. I just thought I should warn you. I'm still your friend, you know. Be careful.

Shock resonates through my body.

It's *worse* than I thought! Panic sets in.

They all know or they're all going to know!

What will happen if my parents see?

How will I explain this?

I try to breathe deeply, realizing I should probably check my other messages. One could be from Ben. I feel a little relief as I see that I'm right, I do have messages from Ben.

Did your lights go out, too?

I'm stunned with realization.

I took out their lights, too?

I drop my phone on my bed and stalk to my bathroom, wanting to check my eyes. I stand gazing in the mirror. They look dark green today, nothing alarming. I sigh with relief, tucking my hair behind my ear. That's when I notice a flash of color in my hair. I furrow my eyebrows and lean in closer to inspect it in the mirror. I untuck my hair and search for the piece. I gasp as I find it and pull it forward.

It's *red*.

There's a *red streak* in my hair.

Not just a hint of the hue, either, it's a vibrant, shocking red.

What. The. Hell.

I jump, suddenly hearing a knock at my window. I peek my head outside of the bathroom, but I can't see anyone from the doorway. I tip toe quietly, dreading who could be waiting for me.

"*Abigail,*" I hear Ben's voice call. "*It's Ben.*" I hear him say.

My body floods with relief at the sound of his voice.

I run to the window, unlock it and slide it open. He climbs in.

"Why didn't you answer me last night?"

"My dad took my phone away. Why aren't you at *school?*" I question him.

"I was *worried* about you. You never *answered* me," he shrugs. "How did everything *go?* Are you okay? You *look*..." he trails off.

I know how I must look, like a crazy person.

"No," I shake my head. "*Nothing* is okay." I run both of my hands through my hair, trying not to rip it all out. I pace my room as Ben watches me. His eyes are wide with alarm. "It went *bad*, Ben. *Everything* is *so* bad." I stop pacing and stand in front of him, grabbing his shoulders. "My dad is *forbidding* me to see you again. But that's not even the *worst* part...my parents want to move *back*. To *Pemberton!* I can't go *back* there, Ben! I'm not *normal* anymore!" My voice rises, in panic.

My hands release him and fall flat at my sides, defeated. Ben looks stunned, his blue eyes are wide.

He swallows. "*No*, you *can't*," he agrees. "I won't *let* you," he enthuses with determination, grabbing my hands in his.

I swallow thickly, gathering courage. "That's actually not the *worst* part *either*, Ben."

He watches me, carefully. "*Say it*, Abby. Tell me what the worst part *is*," he demands.

"They have a *video*," I whisper.

"*Who* does? A video of *what?*" he questions.

"*Everyone*. A video of *me*...in the *cafeteria*. *Everyone's* going to *know*." Tears build in my eyes.

"Bloody hell," he whispers.

Ben pulls me into his arms protectively, holding me fast against his body. I let him hold me up, feeling defeated. "It's going to be *okay*, Abby," he soothes me.

I feel safe in his arms. *He* makes me feel safe.

"*How?*" I look up at him.

"Because we're going to leave." He holds my gaze.

"You and me?" My eyes grow wide.

He nods.

"What about your *brothers?* Are they leaving, *too?*" Panic builds in me, anew.

He shakes his head. "Just us."

I grow silent for a moment. "Ben, I don't want to bring you into *my* mess. *You* don't have to leave. This is your *home.* Yours and your brothers...you're *family*," I argue.

He shrugs. "They'll get over it. Besides, I *own* a cell phone. It's not like they can't call me. Also, *I* dragged *you* into *my* mess. *Remember?* This is all because of *me*," he reminds me.

I don't know what to think.

He wants to run away with me?

But then they'll search for us.

What will happen *if and when* they find us?

What if they try to put Ben in jail for kidnapping?

I wouldn't be surprised if my dad told them that he *did* kidnap me.

What if Ben's right about the authorities, and they try to put me into some sort of government lab?

I shudder.

But what other options did I *have?*

If I stay, I'll be dragged back to Pemberton forever.

Maybe we can just go away for a *little* while?

Until this all boils over?

I can call my parents and let them know I'm safe...

Deep down a voice of intuition tells me that it isn't going to be that simple. Not anymore.

"*Abby*," Ben calls my attention back. "What do you say? Will you run away with me?" he smiles, his blue eyes twinkling.

Who wouldn't?

I sigh. "*Okay,* Ben. But only *temporarily*, just until this all boils over."

He laughs. "Whatever you say, love. You pack a bag, I'm going to get the bike. I'll be right back," he says, beginning to climb back out of the window.

"Bike?" I ask, confused. "We're riding *bikes?*"

He laughs, balancing on the window ledge. "No, silly. We're taking my motorcycle," he winks at me, smiling. Then he hops out of my window.

My mouth drops open.

Motorcycle!

CHAPTER THIRTY-SEVEN
Seattle

I find an old backpack in my closet and begin emptying it, stacking the old folders and spirals underneath my bed. I start to put away the last spiral but pause, wondering if I should leave my mom a note. It seems so cliché...a "runaway" note, but I do it anyway.

Mom, I had to leave town for a little while. Don't worry, I'm safe. I'll keep in contact with you. Don't let dad do anything crazy. I'm NOT being kidnapped. I'm leaving by my own free will. I'll be back before you know it. I love you and dad. Love, Abby.

I tear the note out of the binds and lay it on my already made bed. I sigh as I look down at it, hoping it doesn't break my mom's heart. I realize that Ben will be back soon, so I grab my backpack and start shoving clothes into it. I pack only the essentials: a phone charger, clothes, undergarments, deodorant, a toothbrush and a hairbrush. I don't have much room to pack more, seeing how whatever I pack, I will literally be carrying on my back. I slide my window back closed and lock it. Giving my room a once over, I take one long last look.

I wonder how long I'll be gone?
Where will we go?

I close the door to my room and walk down the hall to my front door. I'm about to leave, when I notice Scout's big fluffy tail flopping around, wagging. She gets up from the spot she was laying at and waits by the door with me. I crouch down to pet her behind her ears.

"Take care of mom and dad for me, okay girl?" I tell her.

I hear the motorcycle pull up and my heart jumps in my throat. I hug Scout and slip out the front door, locking it behind me.

* * *

It's an overcast morning. I check the time and it's only 10:15 a.m. We can get pretty far before anyone will notice. It'll give us a good head start. My mouth dries up at the sight of Ben, sitting on his motorcycle in the driveway. He's wearing a black riding jacket with a matching helmet, jeans and his rugged brown boots.

"You ready?" he calls.

I give him a thumbs up, not able to fully speak yet.

He laughs. "Well, come on then!"

I walk over and stand, staring at him on the motorcycle, not completely sure of how to get on it properly. He senses my apprehension.

"Never been on a motorcycle, have 'ya, love?"

I bite my lip, shaking my head.

"There's a first time for everything," he encourages, handing me the other matching black helmet.

I take it from him and put it on. Then I take a deep breath and climb on behind him, tentatively putting my arms around his waist. He laughs, turning around to say, "you're going to have to hold on tighter than *that*, love." He starts the motorcycle and it growls to life. I immediately tighten my grip around him. He turns around and winks at me. "Don't let go."

We pull out of the driveway and onto the road. My whole body vibrates as we wind through the streets and onto the highway. After a while, I get used to it. The noise of the motorcycle becomes less annoying and more *relaxing*. We reach the highway and I notice that we're leaving Portland.

"So, where are we *going?*" I shout.

"Seattle," Ben shouts back. "I have a friend there that'll let us crash at her place."

I nod.

Her!

He's taking me to a *girl's* house?

Is it his ex-girlfriend or something?

That would be *super* awkward.

Well, at least now I know where we're going.

We stop at a gas station in Olympia to fuel up and get some snacks. I take my phone out to check it while we're in line.

It's only 12:30 p.m.

Lunchtime.

I don't have any missed calls or messages, that's good. No one knows still, or suspects anything. I take a deep, nervous breath. We get back onto the road and before I know it, we're in Seattle. We drive straight into the heart of the Emerald city. We pull up to some pretty swanky looking apartments and into the parking garage. Ben parks his bike and we both get off. My legs feel numb and cramped from riding. I pull the helmet off of my head and set it on Ben's bike. I watch as Ben does the same. His hair is all smashed and messy from the helmet and he looks adorable. I smooth my own hair, wondering what it looks like. For some odd reason, I feel inexplicably shy around him right now, more so than ever. He smirks at me.

"*What?*"

I shake my head quickly.

"Nothing," I mumble, shyly.

He looks at me curiously, then leans forward, making my heart stutter. He reaches into my hair and pulls out the red streak from behind my ear. He twists the piece between his fingers, his eyebrows furrowing in confusion.

"Did you put *red* in your hair?" he asks, a smile playing on his lips.

I know I should tell him the truth, but I can't seem to for some reason. With everything that's been happening, it's just too much.

"Um...yeah. I just wanted to try it out," I lie, hoping he'll believe me.

He seems to though, because his face relaxes.

"*Oh*, cool," he smiles.

I smile back, feeling slightly guilty for lying. He holds out his hand and I take it. We walk over to an elevator and get in. He presses the floor number, seven. We ride in the elevator in awkward silence. I want to ask him who's place this is, but I'm unsure of how to approach it, so I wait. The doors open and we walk out. I notice that the floors in the hall are concrete. Ben leads me down the hall and to a doorway. He knocks on the door.

"Does she *know* you're coming?" I ask, wondering. Ben laughs.

"She *will*."

I feel a frisson of worry run through me.

What if "she" doesn't want me there?

If it's one of Ben's ex-girlfriend's and she's anything like his other ex's, I doubt she'll welcome me with open arms. We wait for a minute and nobody answers. Ben sighs and pulls out his keys.

"She's not home, yet," he mutters.

He selects one and unlocks the door.

He has a key?

This is *not* looking good for me.

I stare at him, surprised. "If you had a key the whole time, then *why*—"

"It's more *polite* to knock," he interrupts me.

He tilts his head at me, smirking. I shake my head at him.

He holds the door open for me. I walk in and scan my surroundings. I realize that her apartment is a loft on the inside. There are no walls separating the rooms, except for the bathroom. Pipes are visible, and run along the brick walls inside. There are a lot of big windows, overlooking a spectacular view of the city. The apartment is decorated modernly, with cultural touches.

This 'friend' must like to travel.

I catch sight of some picture frames and nonchalantly head over to try to get a glimpse of this mystery girl. I'm immediately alarmed when I notice that the brunette in the pictures is striking.

Crap, that's not good.

One of the pictures catches my eye. I walk over to it. It looks older than the others. I lean down to look at it. It's a group of children, four boys and one dark haired little girl. I realize with terror, it's *Ben* and his brothers. All of the boys have dark hair, except for one. I spot Benjamin easily, he stands out with his light hair.

"We were cute little guys back then, weren't we?" I hear his voice in my ear, suddenly. I flinch backward, startled, running into him. He laughs. "Well, I didn't mean to *scare* you."

"I'm fine," I laugh once, embarrassed. "You've known this girl for a *while*, huh?" I comment.

He nods. "We grew up together."

This just keeps getting better and better.

"Come over here. Put your stuff down, get comfortable," he beckons me.

I follow, wondering how I can feel *comfortable* in this *stranger's* apartment. I follow him over to a bed by a window. He sets his stuff down on it and I do the same.

"This is a spare bed, for visitors," he informs me.

How many times has he been here?

He starts to unpack his small bag that he brought. I sit down, nervously. He throws something heavy and metal on the bed, it clinks against his cologne bottle. I reach to pick it up, curiously.

"What's this?" I ask, holding the strange, cold object within my grasp.

"Oh, those are my brass knuckles," he says, nonchalantly.

He takes the object from my hand and tries it on, displaying it for me. Then he does a couple of air punches, showing me how to use them. I gape and try not to show my alarm.

What does he need those for?

He puts them back down. "I'm going to take a shower," he informs me.

He peels off his tight t-shirt right in front of me, showing off his muscular body, on full display. I look away to be polite and he laughs.

He's *much* too good looking up close. I can barely stand it.

He turns around smirking, letting me admire his back while grabbing some things for his shower. I get more of an up-close view of his strange tattoo.

I swallow and ask him. "What is that tattoo of?"

He turns around again, forcing me to stare at his perfect chest and abs. "It's our Irish family crest, we *all* have it," he smiles.

"You *do?*" I ask in surprise. "Yeah," he laughs.

Suddenly, I hear the front door open.

"*Hello?*" A female voice calls.

Dread spreads through me as I watch her walk towards us.

"*Benjamin!*" She gasps, her eyes wide with delight.

He walks over to her shirtless, smiling widely.

"*Lexi!*" he says, warmly.

The Blake Brothers

CHAPTER THIRTY-EIGHT

Sleepover

Just when I thought it couldn't get any worse, "Lexi" steps forward and embraces Ben. I stare at the ground, feeling like I shouldn't be there anymore. Thankfully, she lets go of him after a moment. Her eyes slide from his to face mine. I try to smile, but I'm not sure what it looks like. She smiles back politely, before returning her attention back to Ben.

"What brings you to Seattle, Benjie?" She smiles at him. "And who's your friend?" She winks.

Benjie? Was she *trying* to make me mad?

Ben turns around and holds his hand out to me. I walk forward and take his hand.
"This is my girlfriend, Abby," he smiles, proudly.
A thrill runs through me, hearing him introduce me as his girlfriend for the first time. Lexi looks confused at first, but then holds out her hand for me to shake. I notice with great relief that she's older

than she looks in the photos. She looks more like Max's age, maybe even older. There's also a ruggedness about her that I didn't notice before. She has a delicate nose ring and tattoos on her hands.

"I'm Lexi," she smiles at me, extending her hand to me.

"Nice to meet you," I say, shaking her hand.

"Sorry I didn't call you to let you know that I was coming..." Ben starts.

She smirks at him. "It's fine, you know you're welcome here anytime. What sort of trouble did you get yourself into *this* time?"

The more I hear her talk to him, the better I feel. She speaks to him like he's her kid brother.

He glances at me, smirking. "Actually, *Abby* is the one who needed to hide out for a while," he informs her.

I shoot him an alarmed look. *What* was he doing?

She gazes at me, raising her brow in interest. "*Really*?" she asks.

Ben turns to me and whispers. "It's okay. We don't have to keep any secrets from Lexi. She's an old friend. She knows about...our...*family*."

My eyes bug out of my head.

But how can I trust her with *my* big secret?

"I don't know, Ben, I don't feel *safe* telling anyone else," I whisper back.

Lexi gives us privacy, walking away from us and heading into her small kitchen. She puts down her purse on the counter and digs around in her fridge.

"I wasn't prepared for visitors," she calls. "Looks like we're going to have to order take-out."

An hour later, we're sitting her table, eating Chinese food out of paper cartons. I'm relieved that Ben has put a shirt on now, covering up his too-attractive torso.

I speak up, wanting to break the silence. "So, how do *you* know the Blake brothers?" I ask, curiously.

She swirls noodles onto her fork. "My mom and their aunt were old friends. They used to try to force us to play together when we were little," she smiles fondly, remembering. "But all they ever did was get me into *trouble*," she laughs.

Me and Ben laugh, too.

Ben excuses himself to go to the bathroom, leaving me and Lexi alone. She gazes across the table at me, wondering. A strange look crosses her face.

Loss?

"I used to date Max you know, until things got...*complicated,*" she informs me.

My mouth drops slightly. "I had no idea," I say in surprise. But the longer I look at her, the more it makes sense. She had a certain toughness about her, like Max.

"I figured... I just wanted to clear that up. I didn't want you to think that me and *Ben* had something going on," she laughs.

I laugh, awkwardly. She must've picked up on the vibes I was sending out.

"Ben's more like a little *brother* to me," she says, much to my relief.

I nod.

"So how long have you two been dating?" she asks.

"Not long," I smirk.

"So it's not *serious*, then?" She asks, concern evident in her voice.

That question catches me off guard, at first. We've only been dating for a short time, but our relationship is nothing *but* serious. The risks alone that we take to *be* together makes it that way.

We love each other.

She seems to read my thoughts. "Oh...you *love* him?"

I nod, slowly. She looks stunned.

"But has he told you *about...?*" she asks.

Ben walks up then, joining us. "She *knows* Lexi. That's part of why we're here." She glances at him, then back at me, looking very confused. "Abby *broke* the curse," Ben blurts out, suddenly.

I stare daggers at him, warning him to stop.

Her brown eyes rest on my face. "*But how?*"

Ben shrugs. "She's a witch."

Lexi's eyes bug out of her head.

"*Ben!*" I scold.

I end up explaining the whole story to Lexi who hangs onto every word with dire curiosity.

"Well, that's certainly not your *average* love story," she shakes her head, overwhelmed.

I look out the window, noticing it's already evening. My stomach churns. My parents will be calling soon. As if on cue, my phone rings.

It's my mom.

Both Ben and Lexi turn to look at me. I turn it on silent and wait for the sound of a voicemail. It starts to ring again, this time with my dad's number on the display. I wait for it to finish ringing, before I sigh and turn it off.

Ben reaches over and squeezes my hand. "It'll be fine," he encourages. "You can call them in the morning."

I nod. A few awkward minutes later, *Ben's* phone starts to ring.

"*My* turn," he smiles. "*Hello?*" he answers. I hear yelling on the other side of the line. He holds the phone away from his ear for a moment, telling me on the side. "*Ah,* it's my brother, Max," he jokes, not sounding the least bit surprised. He brings the phone gingerly back to his ear. "*Yes,* I *do* have Abby," he answers Max's unheard question theatrically, smiling at me and looking entertained.

The yelling on the other end of the phone increases, I fight a smile.

Lexi holds out her hand out to Ben, silently asking for the phone. Ben hands it to her, gladly.

"*Hello, Max,*" she purrs. I hear Max pause, then mutter something. "Yes, they're *both* with me," she says, looking at us both. Another pause. "I've been doing *okay.*" Her eyes drop to the floor. "How about *you?*" she asks. She pauses to listen to him, while eyeing us nervously. "Okay, I will. See you *soon,*" she says, hanging up.

Ben and I exchange glances.

"What was that *last* part?" Ben cocks an eyebrow at Lexi.

She sighs. "He and the rest of the gang are coming tomorrow."

Fear grips me, I turn to Ben. "I'm not *ready* to go back yet," I plead.

His eyes look apologetic.

"*Relax*, they're not coming to drag you two back," Lexi says, handing Ben back his phone.

"They're *not?*" Ben seems as surprised as me.

She shakes her head. "They're coming to hide out here for a while, *too*," she says, her eyes wide.

"*What?*" Ben asks, incredulous.

He takes the phone from her and presses the button that I assume must be Max's number. He stands up, pacing as he waits for an answer. As soon as Max answers, he gets straight to the point.

"What's going *on*, Max?" he demands. He pales for a second, before swallowing and smoothing his features. "Are you *sure?*" he asks, his voice lowered to a hushed whisper. "Of course I won't," he answers something Max said, in an annoyed voice. "Right," he says, then hangs up the phone.

I stare at him, even more alarmed than before. "What was *that* about?" I demand.

Ben's eyes look guarded, his mouth sets into a flat line. "We can talk about it *tomorrow*, when they get here." He stands his ground.

I feel panic rising in my chest. I know something's up, and it's bad. Ben wouldn't have reacted that way on the phone if it *wasn't*. I get up and walk over to him.

"But I want to talk about it, *now*," I whisper.

His jaw tenses and his eyes narrow. "We'll *talk* about it tomorrow," he repeats in a low voice, through gritted teeth.

Suddenly, I feel strange, like my powers are wanting to surface. I catch it quickly this time, before the vibration can start.

"*Fine*," I say abruptly, turning away. I turn to Lexi, too angry to look at Ben. "Where can I sleep?"

She looks confused. Ben's voice comes from behind me, and I can literally *hear* the smile in his voice when he says, "with *me*."

I stay turned around, so that he can't see my face heating with embarrassment.

"I'm tired, I'm going to bed," I say to them.

I don't wait for a response this time, instead I turn and walk to the bed where I left my bag, keeping my eyes trained on the ground. I pick up the whole thing and walk to the bathroom, shutting the door behind me.

Once inside, I check my eyes in the mirror, they're glowing again. I sigh to myself, embarrassed. I can hear Ben and Lexi talking in low voices about me through the door. But I don't try to listen to them. I take out my pajamas, change into them and brush my teeth. By the time I'm done in the bathroom, all of the lights are turned off in the loft, except for a few lit candles. I carry my bag through the darkness, wondering where everyone *went*. I spy Lexi on the opposite side of the apartment, lying on her bed. Her TV is on, but it looks like she's already asleep. I walk back to the bed where Ben and I will be sleeping. It's in the corner by the window. My stomach flips as I think of lying next to him all night. I walk up and set my bag down carefully, trying to be quiet. He's lying in the bed in the darkness, I can barely make out his silhouette. I can't see his eyes, so I can't tell if he's awake or asleep. I stand beside the bed for a long moment.

"*Ben?*" I finally whisper.

"*Yes?*" he answers, and I nearly jump out of my skin. I was unaware that he was actually *awake*.

He laughs quietly. "I didn't mean to startle you, love." He sits up. "Now that you're back, I'm going to take that shower that I needed," he says.

I nod.

I'm relieved when he gets his things, leaving me in the bed alone. I watch him walk to the bathroom, turn on the light and close the door. I sigh and lie down, climbing under the covers.

I wonder what my parents are doing?
Have they started a search for me?
I hope they don't hate me for this.

I turn over and try to block all of the thoughts from my head. Before I know it, I fall asleep.

A while later, I'm awakened by the feeling of the bed moving beside me. Benjamin's body slides into the bed, next to mine.

"*Abby, are you awake?*" he whispers.

My eyes fly open.

CHAPTER THIRTY-NINE

Unwelcome

My eyes fight to focus through the darkness, until they land on Ben's face. He's lying on his side, facing me, his face illuminated by the glow of candle light.

I turn to my side, facing him and whisper back. "Yes, I'm awake."

I notice he's not wearing a shirt again and I swallow nervously, secretly wondering what he's wearing for bottoms.

"Good," he smirks. I can feel the heat of his skin from our close proximity. "I wanted to apologize to you for earlier," he starts. "I shouldn't have lost my patience with you. I was frustrated with the *situation*, not you," he explains.

"It's okay..." I mumble. "Tomorrow's almost here. I'll find out soon enough anyway," I smirk, teasingly.

He sighs deeply. "Yeah." A look of worry crosses his features.

"Hey..." I try to distract him. "Worry about it tomorrow," I smile.

"Good idea," he smirks, his usual bad boy behavior returning. He suddenly grabs me by the waist, pulling me dangerously close to his body. I gasp, in surprise. "I've been waiting a long time to do this again," he stares into my eyes.

"Do *what?*" I breathe.

"*Kiss you,*" he says, closing his mouth over mine and kissing me deeply.

I kiss him back just as fervently. His lips trail kisses from the corner of my mouth to my jaw and down my neck. He kisses my collarbone.

"You smell so *good,*" he murmurs.

My breathing is becoming embarrassingly heavy. He looks into my eyes as he starts to trail his hand down my arm, barely skimming my skin, leaving a path of heat where he touches. My hand starts to move, almost by itself. I trail my fingers down his bare chest, hesitantly. His breathing starts to match mine. I reach his stomach and my fingertips skim over the smooth, hard muscles of his six-pack.

He stops my hand with his own. "*Careful, love.*"

"*What?*" I ask, feeling slightly rejected.

"You don't want to start something you can't finish," he warns, smirking.

I feel fear run through my body.

He doesn't mean?

"Besides," he continues. "This isn't the *time* or *place* for that anyway. *Is* it?"

I shake my head vigorously, my eyes wide.

He chuckles. "I'm sorry, I didn't mean to frighten you again." He takes my hand in his, pulling it up to his lips and kissing the top of it. I watch him, wishing he would do it again.

"You *didn't*," I blurt out, embarrassed. But I know he knows the truth.

He smiles. "Good, so I *can* kiss you again?"

"*Yes*," I laugh.

We spend most of the night talking and kissing, eventually we fall asleep in each other's arms.

* * *

I wake to the sound of Ben's phone ringing. I fight my eyes open, realizing that I'm still enveloped in his warm, muscular arms. A huge smile spreads across my face as I recall the events of last night. The sun is already peeking through the window curtains. It's already morning. The phone continues to ring though, and I get worried. I decide I better try to wake him up. I try to turn to face him, but his arms are holding me too snugly.

"Ben," I croak out, much to my surprise. I clear my throat and try again, "*Ben*." I feel him stirring in my arms.

"*Mmmm*," he says.

I giggle. "Ben," I repeat. "Your phone is *ringing*."

"Let it *ring*," he mumbles sleepily, pulling me even closer to his body.

"But what if it's one of your *brothers?* What if it's *important?*" I ask.

As if on cue, Lexi comes stumbling sleepily our way, still wearing her pajamas. "*Ben! Abby!*" she shouts.

We sleepily struggle to sit up.

"What is it, Lexi?" Ben asks, concern etched on his face.

"Max was trying to get a *hold* of you! Him and your brothers are almost here. But there's a *big* problem," she says, breathlessly, her cell phone still in her hand.

"*What is it?* What's the *problem?*" Ben asks, hurriedly.

Her face looks like she'd just seen a ghost. "They're being *followed*," she answers.

"By the *police?*" Ben asks.

She shakes her head. "By Brutus and his boys."

I see Ben's whole posture change at the mention of *that* name. He jumps to his feet immediately, wearing only his boxers.

That's *all* he was *wearing?*

I feel a blush creep onto my face. I try not to stare, but I need to watch Ben's every move. This must be part of what he was going to tell me. Except, I don't think things are going to plan now. He shoves his clothes on, roughly.

"How far?" he asks Lexi, while digging through his bag. He starts laying out various weapons onto the bed that I was unaware that he had. I'm frozen with fear.

"Fifteen minutes," she breathes, her eyes as wide as mine.

He picks his phone up off of the floor and presses Max's number. Max picks up immediately. "I *know.* There's no *time* for that," Ben snaps, annoyed. "You think I *wanted* it this way?" he shouts and I flinch, startled. "Okay, I'll be ready," he hangs up and shoves his phone into his pocket.

He looks at me. "*Get dressed*," he commands. "*We're leaving*."

        I get dressed quickly and grab my bag. We thank Lexi for letting us stay. Before we leave, Ben decides to give her one last piece of advice. "You know, since the curse is broken now, maybe you and Max can...you know...*try again?*" He sounds hopeful. She looks surprised by his words. Ben quickly recovers with. "If we're still *alive* after this," he adds, smirking.

"That's *not* funny," she says. "Have Max call me when you're all *safe*," she sighs.

"I will," Ben promises.

        We get into the elevator and the mood instantly changes. I can feel the tension radiating off of Ben. I almost don't want to ask, but I *have* to. "Ben, what exactly is going *on?*" I turn to face him. "Who's *Brutus?*"

His jaw tenses and he won't look at me, but he answers anyway. "A very bad man," he says, shortly.

I sigh. "Is *he* the reason that your brothers left?" I continue.

He stares at the elevator doors. "*Yes*," he says.

"How do you know *him?* Through your...*work?*" I struggle to say.

"*Yes*," he sighs.

"*Why* are they after you guys?" I feel my heart begin to race, in anticipation of his answer.

He leans against the back of the elevator wall and turns to meet my eyes, finally. "They want *revenge*," he stares into my eyes. "They want to take us *all* down."

I feel the breath being sucked from my lungs. "But, *why?*"

"For what we *did*," he smirks.

"What did you *do?*" I ask, horrified to hear the answer.

"Well," he shrugs. "To be fair, it was mostly my *brothers...* I was sort of *unconscious* at the time. But it was *still* all my fault. Things definitely escalated when they held me hostage for a week."

I feel like I can't breathe. "They're..." I stutter. "They're the ones that *hurt* you?"

If those men were heartless enough to do that to *Ben*, I can only imagine what they would do to *all* of the brothers if they had their chance. He nods.

"What did you guys *do* to them?" I ask. Surely, it couldn't be worse than what *they* had done to *Ben*.

Ben smiles, remembering. "Well, when my brothers rescued me, they waited for the perfect moment, when all of Brutus' men were gone. They knew someone on the inside though, who betrayed Brutus to help us. They rescued me and broke into Brutus' safe. They cleaned out his jewelry collection. There was jewels and diamonds worth millions of dollars in it."

My jaw drops. "*Yeah*, he's sort of pissed about it," he chuckles, darkly.

The elevator doors open and we see the dark SUV parked right next to Ben's bike. Max shouts at us. "Hurry up lovebirds, I don't have all day."

Me and Ben walk quickly over to the SUV, climbing in with the rest of the bunch, leaving Ben's bike behind in the garage. I sit in the back with Ben.

Joseph turns around. "*Ready?*" he asks, a cigarette hanging out of his mouth.

Ben nods, solemnly. Joseph hands Ben his lucky bat and I gulp.

"Alright, Sparky, guess it's time for you to meet some of our *friends*," Max smiles at me through the rearview mirror.

CHAPTER FORTY
Showdown

Just as we're pulling out of the garage, another black SUV pulls up behind us, nearly running into our bumper. This SUV has blacked out windows, the kind that hard criminals have.

"*Shit!*" They've already found us again!" Max yells, pressing his foot down on the gas pedal.

He turns a corner quickly, trying to lose them. But since they're following so closely behind, they keep up easily. The SUV hits their gas, jolting forward and tapping our bumper. It causes everyone in our SUV to jerk forward. Ben grabs me in his arms, holding me protectively.

"*Joseph*," Max orders.

"Yeah, I *got* it," he says casually, pulling out a gun from his waistband.

He unrolls the window and leans out of it. He aims and shoots out one of the tires belonging to the other SUV. The SUV swerves and runs into another car, barely clipping it. Unfortunately, it doesn't slow them down enough. They follow after, zig-zagging behind us. Suddenly, I hear gunshots and glass shattering, as Brutus and his boys return fire. They shoot the back windshield out completely.

"Get *down!*" Ben yells, pushing my head down with his hand.

I do as he says, peeking my eyes up to see if anyone was hit. Much to my relief, nobody was.

"Quinn, get the smoke bombs!" Ben shouts.

Smoke bombs?

Quinn reaches down and grabs a handful out of a bag. He lights them all with a lighter at the same time and tosses them out of the window. I turn and watch them, as they hit the SUV's windshield. Colorful smoke clouds the air behind us, enveloping the SUV. The SUV swerves and spins around, its breaks screech as it comes to a halt. All of the brothers laugh and cheer. We're at least ten miles away from Lexi's house now. Brutus and his boys eventually catch up to us again. Max leads their SUV into an abandoned parking lot on the rougher side of town. He whips the vehicle around, parking. Brutus' SUV pulls up and parks too, facing ours.

Max and his brothers start gathering their weapons.

"*Stay in the car,*" Ben commands. Max passes the keys to the SUV to Ben. Ben takes them and places them in my palm. "If things take a turn for the worst, *leave.*" He stares meaningfully into my eyes. My heart drops into my stomach.

I feel tears building in my eyes. "Do you have to fight them, *right now?* Can't we just lose them somehow? Like *earlier?*" I plead desperately.

Ben shakes his head. "We need to take care of this, now."

"I don't want to *lose* you," I whisper, a tear escaping.

Ben gazes at me mournfully. "You *won't*," he says, brushing the tear away with his thumb.

But I know it's an empty promise. I hear Quinn mutter something that sounds like "sickening", in the background. It makes me remember that they're all still *here*.

Ben made me forget sometimes that other people even *existed* in the world besides us.

"Time to go, Benjamin," Max ordered, solemnly.

Ben gave me a swift kiss. "One more thing," he decided. He pulled a gun from his bag and handed it to me, carefully. "*Just in case.*" His lips mashed into a serious line. I hold onto the gun like it's a snake, deadly and poisonous. I don't know how to *shoot* a gun, nor do I want to *learn*. I'd never supported the use of the steel killing machines. I can't imagine what I'd *do* if I was left with the decision of killing someone to save *my* life, *or* someone else's. I don't think I would have the guts to pull the trigger. Even *if* it was on a dangerous criminal. I look up to see Brutus and his men getting out of their SUV. I know immediately which one is *Brutus*. He makes Max look like a regular Joe. He's tall and at least three times as brawny as Max. His black hair is clipped short and he has a dark five o'clock shadow. Three other guys are with him, ranging in different ages and builds. They all look equally as mean, but *none* of them are as scary as *Brutus* himself. The look in Brutus' eyes chilled me to the bone. It was the look of a cold-hearted killer. The look of a man who's lost the ability to *feel* a long time ago. The look of a man without a *soul*.

Max, Ben, and his brothers all file out of our vehicle, too. They close the door behind them, leaving me alone in the SUV. I creep to the middle of the vehicle and peek from behind the seats, keeping myself obscured. I have a direct view of what's happening from the windshield.

They don't know that I'm here.

In a way, that's an advantage. That's if, I figure out a way I can *help*.

I train my eyes to Ben and his brothers. Brutus' men and the Blake brothers all start conversing, like old friends. I'm confused at first, until Brutus unexpectedly pulls a knife, stabbing Max square in the stomach. Max falls to the floor, grasping his stomach.

I feel like time slows down, as terror grips me.

It all happens in slow motion. Joseph screams, tackling Brutus and they struggle on the floor, fighting over the knife. Quinn pulls a knife of his own, stabbing one of the men. Ben picks up his bat and swings, knocking out another. Leaving one man free to attack. I watch him, as he slowly approaches Ben from behind. He pulls a gun and points it to the back of Ben's head.

A deafening scream escapes my mouth.

The remaining glass in the SUV's windows, shatters. Everyone stops and turns to see what's happening. The vibration fills my body faster than it *ever* has, shaking the entire SUV. *This time,* I know *exactly* what to do with it. With shaking hands, I drop the gun that Ben gave me. I won't be needing it. Opening the door to the SUV, I step out.

"Who the hell is *this?* Your *girlfriend?*" The man with the gun asks.

"That's *Sparky*," Max coughs, still lying on the ground. "She's with *us*," he adds.

"Well, *Sparky*. Which one of these *idiots* is your boyfriend? I want to kill *him* first." The man threatens.

I ignore his comment, walking slowly towards him and trying to stay focused. "Put the gun *down*," I warn him.

"What the hell is wrong with her *eyes?*" He asks nervously, suddenly noticing. The gun is trembling in his hands.

Quinn wipes off his knife. "She's a witch," he says, matter-of-factly.

Quinn's almost bored tone causes all of the men to erupt in raucous laughter.

"*Move*, you guys," I tell Ben and his brothers. "I don't want you to get *hurt*."

Ben's eyes are huge, but he and his brothers actually *listen* to me. Joseph drags Max away.

Brutus gets up off of the floor. "Is this some sort of *joke*, Max? You *know* my patience level," he warns.

I note that he has a thick foreign accent.

The guy knocked out by Ben, remains lying on the floor. The guy stabbed by Quinn though, stumbles to his feet, ready to fight again. The one with the gun, points it at my head instead. I smile at him, then lift my hand in the direction of the gun and point at it. An electric shock escapes my fingers, zapping the gun from his hand. Then I wave my hand backward, sending the weapon flying into the trees behind us. A look of fear crosses the man's features. Brutus runs at me next. I lift both of my hands and *push* him away, knocking him backward with *way* more force than I thought I was capable of. Brutus' body lands onto their SUV with a sickening thump and the sound of glass buckling.

My battle against Brutus' men continues as the power shoots out of my fingers like volts, shocking the men one by one as they attempt to attack me. They looked like they're being electrocuted, the way their bodies jolt around in an unnatural way as I struck them. One by one, I take away the men's weapons. Eventually, they all give up and run back into their SUV. Minus the man who was still knocked out on the ground. They leave him behind.

"This isn't *over!*" Brutus yells, before climbing back into his SUV.

It's comical to watch the way the brutes retreat back into their SUV, like dogs with their tails between their legs.

"Yes it is," I mutter to myself.

I wasn't finished with them yet. I lifted my hands again. This time I lifted the *whole* SUV at least five feet off of the ground. I could hear Brutus and his men yelling expletives from the inside. Spinning it slowly, I threw it backwards, like it was a toy car. It rolled a few times, before landing with a loud crash of crushed metal and shattered glass. I watched as it bursted into flames. Two of the men make it out in time by retreating on foot.

But not Brutus.

We watch as flames engulf the entire vehicle, incinerating it.

"*Damn*," Joseph says, mirroring everyone's thoughts with one word.

I wipe the smile off of my face, remembering suddenly.

I turn around. "Where's Max?"

The brothers move aside, and I see Max lying on the floor, looking more pale than usual. I stride over to him, crouching beside him. I lift his bloody shirt up, revealing a deep gash in the middle of his stomach. I gasp and swallow hard, feeling sick and cold at once. Blood is oozing too quickly out of the wound.

"What do you think Sparky, you still got that *sewing kit?*" he choked out, trying to be funny.

I shook my head. "You're going to need more than *that* for *this*, Max."

"*Fix him*, Abby," I hear Ben say.

I look up at him in shock. His eyes are desperate, but determined. Joseph nods encouragingly, and Quinn glances skeptically at his brothers.

I'd never *thought* of that.

What if my powers weren't *all* bad?

I *did* heal my own wound once. *Unintentionally*, of course.

Could I do it *again?*

To someone *else?*

"I'll *try*," I swallow, nervously.

I concentrate as I lift my hands once more, waving them slowly over Max's stomach. I close my eyes and try my hardest, afraid that I might accidentally *hurt* him instead. When I hear what sounds like *positive* whispering and gasps coming from the brothers, I squint my eyes open. The wound slowly begins to heal. I watch in disbelief as it *completely* seals back up.

Max makes a startled strange sound as he watches. "*Oh, my...What the?...How the..?*" he stutters, dumbfounded.

"You *did* it," Ben whispers in wonder.

I pull my hands away, breathing heavily. Then I fall over, too dizzy to sit up anymore.

"*Abby!*" Ben shouts, as I come to rest on the concrete. He rushes over to me, picking me up and cradling me in his lap. "Are you *okay?*" he presses his palm to my forehead. His hands feel warm against my cold skin.

I laugh. "Just a little... *weak*. Can you get my phone, Ben?" I ask.

"Sure, why do you need it?" he asks, his voice soft.

"I need to call my mom," I say.

CHAPTER FORTY-ONE

EPILOGUE

It's been two weeks since the incident with Brutus and his boys, even though it still feels like yesterday.

The memories were all still fresh in my mind. I realize now, how lucky I am that I was able to use and control my powers so well when I needed them the most. It was the first time that had *ever* happened to me. It couldn't have happened at a *better* time. It was like some sort of *miracle*. Whenever I think about what could've happened to Ben and his brothers if I wasn't there to help that day, I shudder to myself.

It would've been the end of the Blake brothers.

I called my parents to let them know that I'm safe. I knew it would help for them to hear my voice. I tried to convince them that I *wasn't* with Ben and his brothers, but they knew better. I told them I would stay in touch. To call off the search, but my dad refused. I had to trash my cell phone, since they would only use it to track me anyway. Ben got me a new one that was untraceable.

We'd stayed in Seattle. I'm glad my parents didn't know *that*. Max said it worked well because no one would expect us to be so *close*. We occupied run-down hotels and crashed with more of Ben's brothers' "friends" for a while. Until one day, we finally found a place to stay. A "safe house" as Ben calls it. It's actually just an abandoned house that Max found. So technically, we're just squatters. Max insisted on us all returning to school, even though I wasn't sure how we could "lay low" while doing so. He said that the *last* thing people would expect a bunch of teenage runaways to *do* is enroll back in *school*. I guess he wasn't completely off.

We were sitting in the living room, watching the small TV that Max found while dumpster diving one day. The news report came on again, similar to the ones I'd seen before, since we left Portland.

"The search continues for a missing teenage girl from Portland, Oregon. Sixteen-year-old Abigail Brooks was reported missing two weeks ago."

My school picture flashed onto the screen.

"It is believed that she is traveling with four teenage brothers. Max, Joseph, Quinn and Benjamin Blake, who have also disappeared from their Portland home."

All of their school pictures flashed onto the screen next, lined up in order from oldest to youngest.

"When authorities searched the boys' home, they found their legal guardian, Adeline Gardener, buried in their backyard. According to forensic pathologists, the body had been there for over a

year. The Blake brothers are now the prime suspects in her murder. It is believed that Abigail is in extreme and immediate danger. If anyone has any details regarding her disappearance, they are to alert authorities immediately."

I get up and turn off the TV, annoyed. "It's just like I thought it would be. I'm the 'victim' and you guys are the 'kidnappers'," I sigh.

"Don't forget murderers," Max pointed out.

Ben shot him a pointed look. Max's cell phone buzzed and we all look at it at once. Max picks it up and smiles. He slid over the screen and started typing something with a goofy look on his face.

Joseph rolls his eyes.

"*Lexi* again," He answered all of our unspoken questions.

Quinn scoffs. "The Blake brothers are all going *soft*," he complains.

The brothers look so strange with their bleach blonde hair. They had to bleach it to change their appearance. Part of our new "identities".

Except for Ben.

Since his hair is naturally so light, the only choice was to go *darker*. His hair is now dyed a dark, chocolate brown. I don't mind it though, it just makes his brilliant blue eyes stand out even more. Max is even growing his hair out to make an effort, as well. A black, fuzzy stubble has started to surface on the top of his head.

I have a disguise of my own. It wasn't a hard decision, my hair was naturally changing on its own anyway. The day after I had used so much of my powers, I woke up with more startling red streaks in my hair. I couldn't hide it from Ben anymore, he knew I didn't have time to go to the *salon*. I realized the more I was using my powers, the more red my hair was turning. So, naturally, I dyed my hair red. With my now permanent green eyes and red hair, I looked like a *totally* different person than the picture they had put on the news.

I *felt* like it, too.

Max had gotten the glass fixed on the SUV and had it painted *gold*, of all colors. He also got the plates changed on it, too. It certainly was convenient that Max had so many "connections". They had all played a part in helping us, no matter how "shady" they may have been.

I heard what sounded like a strange commotion coming from Quinn's phone. Curiously, I walked over and peered over his shoulder to see what it was. He was so absorbed in what he was watching, that he doesn't notice my approach. When I realized just what it was that he was watching, I gasped. It's the video of *me* in the cafeteria, the one I'd heard was going around. Quinn, realizing what he'd done, turned it off immediately and put his phone away. But it was too late, the damage was already done. I'd already saw it.

It was titled "mutant girl" and it already had two million hits.

"*Dammit*, Quinn! What did I *tell* you about that?" Ben said angrily.

"You can't protect her *forever*, Ben! She needs to know the truth anyway," Quinn responded defensively.

"He's *right*," I sighed. Ben looked wounded. "This *is* my life now," I said, sounding more depressed than I intended to.

Max came over cheerfully. "Well, I enrolled everyone for school tomorrow, it's *all* taken care of. We all have new names and identities, don't *forget* that. We'll all be attending Emerald Skies High."

The next day, we pulled up to our new high school. Saying I was nervous would be an understatement. The brothers have to drop me off at the curb to avoid being seen with me. The new rules are as follows: pretend that we don't know each other, and *never* be seen together. We'd have to be very careful now, of how we communicated while on school grounds.

"Good luck, Sparky," Max calls.

"Thanks," I mumble.

"See you inside." Ben winks at me and gives my hand a reassuring squeeze.

I hop out and walk across the front lawn, feeling like a giant red target. I make it inside and into the office with no problem. A woman with a messy, blonde bun greets me.

"How can I help you?" she smiles.

I push up my fake, thick, black-framed glasses, also a part of my "disguise". I'd definitely have to get used to them, but at least they helped me to camouflage my unnaturally green eyes.

"I'm new here and I need to pick up my schedule, please," I smile.

"Yes of course," she digs into a file. "What's your name, dear?"

"Scarlet Night," I say, adjusting to the sound of it.

I had to come to terms with it. I know that it was just supposed to be a "fake" new identity, but to be truthful, I *wasn't* the same person anymore. I had changed too much to go back to being the person I used to be...I didn't even know who she was anymore.

As far as I was concerned, Abigail Brooks was gone.

LISTEN TO THE PLAYLIST!

Want to hear the music that inspired the book? The Blake Brothers Spotify playlist link is below! Give it a listen! Or look it up on Spotify by its name:

The Blake Brothers

WHAT'S NEXT!

Continue The Blake Brothers series with:

Scarlet Night (book 2)
&
The Curse of Everly Jones (book 3)

Available on Amazon Kindle and paperback now!

MORE BOOKS BY KATHEY GRAY!

<u>Young Adult Fantasy Series:</u>

(The Blake Brother series)
Scarlet Night - book 2
The Curse of Everly Jones - book 3

<u>Chick-Lit/ Romance Books:</u>

Breaking Girl Code
Burning The Rules
(Series)

&

One Drunk Text (Standalone)

<u>Dark Romance/ Thriller:</u>

He Loves Me...
He Loves Me Not

Poetry Books:

Real Shit & Pretty Words
Muted Thoughts

Anthologies:

Tales Around The Supper Table
The Invisible Train (Short Story- Middle Grade Fiction)

More About This Author:

Kathey's   Website:
https://hlywood21.wixsite.com/katheygray
Kathey's   Amazon   Author   Page:
https://www.amazon.com/Kathey-Gray
Goodreads:
https://www.goodreads.com/author/show/Kathey_
Gray
Facebook:
https://www.facebook.com/authorkatheygray
Instagram:
https://www.instagram.com/theunstoppablemrs.gra
y/
Twitter: @unstoppablegray